DANCER
DAUGHTER
TRAITOR
SPY

DANCER
DAUGHTER
TRAITOR
SPY

ELIZABETH KIEM

Published in the United States by Soho Teen
an imprint of
Soho Press, Inc.
853 Broadway
New York, NY 10003

This is a work of fiction. Any resemblance of characters to actual persons, living or dead, is purely coincidental. Winged Guitars, however, is based on the author's fond regard for the group ДДТ, who still make music today.

Kiem, Elizabeth, 1970–
Dancer, daughter, traitor, spy / by Elizabeth Kiem.
    p cm
ISBN 978-1-61695-263-1 (alk. paper)
eISBN 978-1-61695-264-8
1. Spies—Fiction. 2. Clairvoyance—Fiction. 3. Russian
Americans—Fiction. 4. Soviet Union—Relations—United States—Fiction. 5.
United States—Relations—Soviet Union—Fiction. 6. Brooklyn (New York,
N.Y.)—History—20th century—Fiction. I. Title.
PZ7.K54Dan 2013
[Fic]—dc23 2013006502

Interior design by Janine Agro, Soho Press, Inc.

Printed in the United States of America

10 9 8 7 6 5 4 3 2 1

Дяде ТК

PART ONE
MOSCOW NOVEMBER 1982
MUSIC AT THE END OF AN ERA

ONE
TCHAIKOVSKY

November dusk slips into Moscow like a spy; you don't know it's there until it has stolen the day and vanished into the dark. But on the night that my mother disappears from my life, I could swear that I see it happen. The arrival of twilight, I mean—not my mother's disappearance. That's something I don't see coming. Not until it is too late. Not until she's already gone.

VERA PETROVNA HAS JUST called us to center when the first streetlamp snaps on at the top of the boulevard. I linger at the barre watching the wrought-iron lamps cast halos, one after the other, against the opposite brick wall. Like an electric *corps de ballet*, dusk is making its entrance onto Theater Square.

Vera Petrovna, imperious in her loose caftan, raps her stick on the wooden floor. "Marina," she barks. "Will you be joining us?"

I hurry to the center—to my place in the first row. I take fifth position, shift into a fourth position preparation, and execute a triple pirouette.

Vera Petrovna nods. She places both hands on her stick and leans forward slightly, like she might be passing gas.

"Again," she says.

Fifth to fourth, and another triple turn. Then another and another. I land each one perfectly. So does each of the dancers in Vera Petrovna's advanced repertory academy of the Bolshoi Ballet, class of 1982.

There is no clock in the high-ceilinged studio. But we spend a precise number of minutes in this room, six days a week. They are measured in *tendus*, *frappés*, and *fouettés*. Barre exercises last twenty-five minutes. Center combinations are given in ten, reversed for seven, repeated in groups of three for thirteen minutes; turns in the center for eight; turns from the corner for five; reversals and a combination for fifteen; leaps fill ten more minutes without an *allegro*; *adagio* combinations and *port de bras* add ten. A five-minute break comes either before or after the jumps. We stretch for another ten minutes once class is dismissed. The only thing that alters this pattern from week to week is when (relative to the barre and the break and the *port de bras*) the streetlights come up on the boulevard.

Some nights, the puddles of streetlight through the lace curtains are large enough to swallow all your concentration. The day should be done. All over the city, fathers are descending into the metro, and mothers are inching closer to the front of the line to pay for the *pel-meni* for dinner.

Not *my* mother, of course. She has a car and a driver. Tonight's meal is being prepared as always by our bossy housekeeper, Ludmila Alekseevna, who sings gypsy ballads as she beats the shit out of a piece of pork and pleads with my mother to get "one of those merciful Bulgarian meat grinders."

That's the beauty of our so-called Socialist Paradise. The unity of our Soviet Union. We may be past the "collective" craze when we all shared a cow and a tractor and a kitchen sink, but we still share a superficial reality. Everyday life is pretty much the same for us all, and so the deeper essence is, too. They want it to be Communism. But what it is, really, is Commonism. Twilight might catch us unaware, but its arrival makes all us Soviets—comrades and *komsomols*, hoodlums and cranks—think of courtyards full of kitchen light, the smell of chicken cutlets and tea, and the clarion of the radio announcing that it is eight o'clock, Moscow time.

Tonight, for me and the rest of the girls midway through their *temps lie,* eight o'clock looms larger than usual. Because tonight they will announce the winner of the All-Union Debut Prize on *Youth Estrada.* We will find out, all together, shortly after eight o'clock Moscow time, if it's the Latvian Handsomes or our own favorite group, Winged Guitars.

We finish the center combination, and Vera Petrovna tells us to take five. I'm just coming out of the bathroom when I overhear Anya whispering to Dasha. "At

least she'll make sure Danilov gets back on the plane."
Then she sees me and winks, ignoring the daggers in
my eyes.

"Anya," shouts Vera Petrovna from where she stands
by the piano. "A chatterbox cannot be a soloist."

Anya's cheeks flush red. She lifts her chin and crosses
the floor in a fully extended *tour jeté cabriole*, landing
with a dramatic *developé* into *pas de bourrée* and a toss
of her head.

"But they make good gymnasts," says Vera Petrovna
acidly.

Anya is one of Vera Petrovna's most talented students,
and I'm not just saying that because she's my best friend
in the academy. Or because people always think that we
can't truly be friends because we're both aspiring ballerinas in the Soviet Union's most prestigious company.
Anya has been dancing since she was six years old. My
mother didn't start me in classes until I was nine. She
says her own challenges as a young ballerina made her
question whether she should "inflict" such a fate on
her daughter. She says she only gave in because I was
very insistent. And because one night I put on Ludmila
Alekseevna's hard-toed clogs and performed half of the
"Dance of the Little Swans" in the parquet foyer.

"DO YOU THINK I didn't hear that?"

Vera Petrovna has finally dismissed us and Anya is
sitting in the corner unwinding tape from her toes, gin-
gerly peeling each bloody digit from its neighbor. Her
shoes are new and not broken in.

"Hear what, sweetie?" she asks, craning her neck up at me.

"'At least she'll make sure Danilov gets back on the plane.' What was that supposed to mean?" I ask, though I know exactly what it was supposed to mean.

Anya stands and puts her arm around my shoulders. "Marya," she says quietly. "Don't listen to what I say. I'm only saying it so that you don't have to. You don't have to listen to what any of them say. Dasha, Vika, Tatiana—they love to pretend that your mother is only invited on the American tour because Arkady Grigorievich Danilov is in love with her."

"She's also a favorite abroad," I say in her defense. "And she's not a flight risk."

"Of course," nods Anya. "But that doesn't change the fact that Arkady Grigorievich *is*, in fact, in love with her. And he's the director. And, also, is going on tour himself. So just let me acknowledge it. That way you don't have to."

We've drifted to the far side of the studio where the ashen-faced pianist is packing up his music, an unlit cigarette already in his mouth. I look back at the other girls sprawled in the center, laughing and talking. Dasha is up against the mirror, brushing out her thick auburn hair and making kiss lips at herself. Tatiana is contorting herself into thoroughly unclassical positions in an effort to examine her ass from behind, as opposed to *en eleve*, or from the silhouette of an *attitude derriere*.

You might think that, being forced to watch ourselves in the mirror on a daily basis for hours on end, we'd have a pretty good idea what we look like. Well, we still flock to our reflections for a closer inspection. There is no creature as narcissistic as a teenage ballerina. Unless it's a prima donna looking her fortieth birthday in the face, like my mother. I recall a snatch of conversation between my parents last night that wasn't meant for me to hear:

"*Sveta, think of Marya. She's seventeen. Think what you are asking. She has too much to lose.*"

"*What can we know about that? Really? I've done what I can, Vitya. And I know what others have done to bring us to this point. I know it with certainty. And that's all I have to act on.*"

"*It's too soon.*"

"*No. It's time.*"

I don't know what Pop was urging her patience with last night, but if it has to do with me and with my mother, it's about the ballet. And if it has to do with the ballet, it will happen on my mother's own timeline.

I slide into a split and run through my stretches in silence.

"Tell me the truth," I ask Anya once the others have left to change into their street clothes. "Do you think it should be Olga Dmitrievna who's going as cultural emissary and not my mother?"

Anya laughs. "I think it should be *me* who's going."

There's a shriek outside the studio. "Whose *dublonka*?"

I follow Anya into the antechamber we use as a dressing room and find Tatiana enveloped in my new coat: a beautiful knee-length plum-colored suede not yet found in the shops.

"Yours, Marina? Oh my god can you get me one? It's so yummy! Of course, I'd need one size smaller." Tatiana fingers the fur ruff at the collar and sleeve, unties the sash, and examines the neat lining for foreign labels. "Is it ours?" she asks, meaning Soviet-made. "Let's see it on you—the color is so unusual."

I model the *dublonka* graciously. "A gift to my mother," I explain. "I don't remember who from. Anyway, my mother doesn't think it suits her. She said I can wear it for the winter."

Tatiana's eyes narrow slightly. "Well it's just lovely on you, Marya. But don't let whoever gave it to your mom see you in it. That might be, let's say, awkward."

Another veiled reference. Even after a decade as the Bolshoi's principal female, no dancer would expect her star not to fade. But my mother is no ordinary ballerina. Svetlana Dukovskaya is not just gorgeous, graceful, and unsurpassed in technique. She's a globally recognized personality. The West can't get enough of her. Our Ministry of Culture fans the flame of her fame, squiring her about on international tours. After all, who else do we have to help win our celebrity Cold War against America? Chess masters are not terribly charismatic. Our writers are either hermits or boors. We haven't had a cute cosmonaut since Yuri Gagarin. Our best musicians are kept in basements and miniscule theaters because our authorities don't approve of rock and roll. It's "degenerate capitalist dreck." (Except for Winged Guitars, that is. Winged Guitars write lyrics the authorities don't fully understand, and they play unplugged. Our Supreme

Soviet hates electronic music. "Bourgeois *shum*," they call it.)

Anyway, my mother has been given certain freedoms— as an artistic trophy, a cultural emissary. She no longer performs, but she is still a diva. And she's something of an insurance policy. She's loyal, I remind Anya. A true "cultural patriot of the Motherland." She ensures that the Bolshoi director, Arkady Grigorievich Danilov—who has his own ties to the West—won't be following the lead of those other Bolshoi greats. Those dancers whose names we no longer mention because they have traitorously slunk off to Western embassies in the middle of their tours. The ones who betrayed the Motherland for fame. Sure, some say it was for freedom. Others say for cocaine. I say there is nothing worth betraying the Bolshoi Ballet. Sveta has taught me that.

Another thing about my mother? She expects me to step into her shoes.

She's seventeen, my father said. *It's too soon.*

But he knows nothing of the ballet. Or next to nothing.

Anya has pulled her skirt and sweater over her tights and is racing to catch up with the girls who will catch the bus at Kitai Gorod. She gives me a peck on the cheek. "Call me tonight? When *Youth Estrada* comes on?" she says, and she's gone. Tatiana and Vika change more leisurely, taking forever to adjust their knit hats just so. Then they kiss me goodbye, too, leaving a smear of lipgloss on my cheek. Now I'm alone in the dressing room.

I take a seat on a chair that hasn't been upholstered since the theater's jubilee some thirty-five years ago and study the portraits of the Bolshoi's leading ladies. Pavlova as the Dying Swan; Baranova as a spurned bride; Bessmertnaya in a feathered headdress . . . Three rows of ballerinas in classical poses: eyes mournful, legs joyful, hands expressive, lips rouged, and brows plucked into ironic expressions of grace.

The last portrait is of my mother, a soft-focus beauty with wide-set eyes and dark hair like mine. Her back is to the camera, and she is laughing over her bare shoulder. For the first time I realize that this is not an official portrait at all. The one that hangs in the *parterre* and is printed in all the bulletins is of Svetlana in her signature role of Coppélia. This is not it. This is a relaxed, candid shot. I can imagine it taken on the beach in the Baltics. Or in Gorky Park by the carousel. Or at our *dacha*, where my mother spends hours bedding flowers that never survive the winter. I can imagine my father hunkered low in the weeds with his camera: "*Sveta. Sveta, ulibnis.*" *Sveta, smile.* As if she would do anything else with a camera trained on her.

I bend to pull on my boots. They are real leather, tight to the calf with a two-inch heel, very stylish. As I'm zipping up the left, my hair falls over my eyes like a curtain. I become aware of a sudden silence. As though I have entered a pressure chamber and left the outside world of sound. I straighten up, dizzy. Another curtain descends: a gauzy screen between me and the wall of portraits. I feel the onset of tunnel vision and lean back in the chair to steady myself. My eyes are closed. But I am still seeing the wall—only at the far end of a long hallway.

The door opens and a figure enters. He stands with his back to me, studying the portraits. I watch him as he places his hands on my mother's photograph and removes it. He seems to be polishing it, handling it with loving care, but a voice in my head says, *erasing it.*

Then, without warning, he raises it above his head and throws it to the ground. Curiously I don't hear the glass shatter. But such an act, such violence, produces damage, no? After a moment I rise and stagger toward the wall. It takes too long, as if I'm crippled or swimming in space. By the time I reach the wall, the figure is gone. But the photograph lies on the floor. The glass is broken, and I can see that my mother's face also is . . . cracked. Wrinkled. Old. Her exposed back is spotted with age. Her long hair is grey. She is still looking at me over her shoulder, and she is still smiling. But the smile has lost its brilliance.

I heave air into my lungs like a girl plucked from drowning. I find myself standing with one foot shod like a half-peeled banana, my mother's cracked portrait at the toe.

My palm is bleeding. Stumbling to the sink, I hold it under the tap, watching the basin fill with pink water. Finally my heart stops racing. I pull a long bandage from my dance bag and wrap my hand just as I would a strained ankle. Somehow I manage to zip the boots up with one hand swaddled. I grab my coat and bag and shoot out into the hallway, headed for the exit, blinder than usual to the faded opulence of the grand foyer that once witnessed the coronations of czars. I'm almost to the door when I hear a man's familiar high-pitched voice behind me.

"Stop one moment, Marina."

There is no one I want to see less than Danilov at this moment. I'm desperate to be free of the theater.

"Is your mother picking you up?" he asks. He sees the confusion on my face. "It's Wednesday, and I know you and your mother usually go home together on Wednesday, but since she missed the union meeting . . . it's quite important that I speak with Svetlana immediately." He tugs his neat, trim beard. "She also missed a rather important appointment with the Minister this morning, and I need to brief her." I'm still struck dumb. "I've left a message with your housekeeper. But please do ask her to call me."

I find my voice. "I'll do that, Arkady Grigorievich. Good night."

"Good night, Marina. You look quite fetching in that coat, by the way."

I push my whole weight against the heavy door and flee.

THE COLD AIR IS a relief. I wrap my scarf tighter and stand in front of the theater, considering. Sveta, it seems, has left me to get home on my own. It's not the first time. Just like it's not the first time I've had a strange vision that is clearer than day. These things happen to me. I have these . . . spells. So does my mother. I don't worry so much about them. I think of them as a necessary evil inherent to ballet. Like being a smoker or being a shade too skinny. Like a life without fashionable short hair-cuts. True—this one was, perhaps, a bit stronger than past episodes, in that it was all vision and no blackout. But I'm not ready to analyze it yet. We are taught to dismiss Freud as bourgeois psychology, so why should I be upset by visions of my mother as an old woman? Easier to be annoyed that she's not here to drive me home.

Home is the *vysotka* on Krasnopresnya, an elite address in one of the seven so-called "Stalinscrapers" that you can pick out from most anywhere in Moscow. They are about five times taller than any other building and built after the war when our Great Leader, Joseph Stalin, decided that without American-style skyscrapers, the Soviet Union couldn't fully enjoy its victory. So he rounded up all the German prisoners of war, the country's best architects, and all the steel and cranes within 500 kilometers, and built the *vysotki*, the craziest damn skyscrapers you've ever seen. Forget the Empire State Building; that's just one lonely tower at a flat cross-roads. Our "Stalinscrapers" roam across hillsides and squat across swamps and riverbeds. They have multiple turrets, each with a dozen entrances, elevator banks, pinnacles and pilasters, cornices and plinths . . . I think those are the right terms, but I'm not a student of architecture. They are all a little different, but they are all the same: gigantic sandcastles built by a lunatic. Except they won't wash away.

Around me the evening rush is in full stream and I realize that what I really want is to join it, to melt into the crowd. A guy on the corner is tugging on the sleeve of a girl my age, hatless and laughing. *"Kuda ti?"* he is asking. *Where are you going?* He's awfully cute, the guy, and I'm half jealous of the girl. *"Domoy!"* she laughs, and then she kisses him. *Home.* Me too, I think. *Ya hochu domoy.*

I can take the metro and be home before Pop, but from the theater I can see the top of my building, and I know that I will walk. The night is icy crystal. I join the mass and their moving conversation:

"Not likely, Vera. I haven't seen canned eggplant since spring . . ."

"Get stuffed! You think I don't remember that weekend?"

"We'll just have to see how the Committee decides . . ."

"A red Niva with a broken taillight . . ."

"Something's wrong. Look at the guards."

I stop in the middle of the sidewalk across from the entrance to Red Square, surprised to see the entryway blocked by a tank, something you see on the square only on holidays and parade days. A cluster of soldiers stands next to it. They seem much more formal than the usual sentries. There's a palpable wariness that stops me in my tracks.

Why do I feel certain that at any moment the Kremlin walls and illuminated towers will collapse, like my mother's phantom portrait? I don't know; it's like that sometimes after one of my episodes. Like when you wake up from a strange dream and it seems to evaporate even as you are trying to remember it. Only the opposite: these dreams I have when I'm awake? It's as though it takes time for them to settle into some space in my brain that I recognize as my own. And while they are taking root there, I see them everywhere else. In the star-topped towers of the Kremlin. In the street lamps. In the glass storefront full of women in shapeless winter coats. I see my mother's picture shatter in each of them.

At the end of the wall, cars are streaming across the bridge to Moskvarechie. That's where we go on weekends, me and my friends, to dance parties or art shows at the House of Youth or the Artist Café . . .

A traffic cop whistles sharply and I stumble back. He yells and gestures to the underground crosswalk. But I don't want to go down there, where the air reeks of vodka and wet cardboard, and it echoes with kids who worship the Sex Pistols and Viktor Tsoi, the kids who wear safety pins in their ears and toilet flush chains around their neck.

I'm halfway down Kalininsky when the car pulls up beside me.

"Marina," shouts Oleg, leaning over the passenger seat to roll down the window. "Jump in, I'll take you home." I duck under the guardrail and open the door. The car smells, as always, of my mother's perfume.

"What happened?" I ask.

Oleg offers a gruff shrug. "Svetlana said she wouldn't need me till evening. Said that in the morning. That she'd need me later. In the evening. So it's evening, isn't it? If she needs me, I don't know where. She didn't say where she'd need me. Just later. Evening. But not where. So I goes to the house. Then I goes to the theater. Don't know where she needs me. But hey, here you are. Huh, Marya?"

By the time our driver has finished his monologue we're already home. He pulls up in front of our building. I clatter across the cavernous foyer, greeting the old woman on duty at the concierge desk. Ten of these fierce old *babas* take shifts, scrutinizing anyone coming or going. But they are as familiar and harmless as the ceramic pigs on our bookshelves.

When the elevator opens onto our landing, Dyadya Gosha is standing before me.

"Marya, *privyet*," he says, looking me up and down. His eyes are bloodshot, and there's two days of grey stubble on his cheeks. "Your pop's home, hurry up. He's waiting for you."

Something about his greeting strikes me as strange. Georgi, Uncle Gosha, hurries off like he has somewhere to be. He's not really my uncle, Dyadya Gosha. Pop's brother died before I was born. But Georgi Levshik has been my father's best friend forever. They've been together for it all: pioneer camp, first hangovers, the army, the institute, marriage, divorce. And now, I know, they're growing apart. Because Gosha won't accept what my father has—everything. Because Gosha thinks there is even more.

"Where have you been?"

My father steps out of the kitchen. He looks harried, and I can tell he's been manhandling both his hair and his tie.

I breathe in the comforting November smell of borsht, fried potatoes, and floor polish. "Walked home.

Ma wasn't at the theater, so . . ." I pull off my boots and *dublonka* and slip into the bathroom. The bandage has a thin red streak so I remove that too and wash my hands. The cut is clean. The hot water stings.

In the kitchen Ludmila Alekseevna is muttering as she places dishes on the table and ladles soup into bowls. "No good reason. What business does he have? He needs to let himself in like the cook herself? Has he come to make dinner, no? Just *v'gosti*, he says. 'For a visit.' Come for a visit when someone's home, I say. And then, the scoundrel, all sweetness, 'but you're home, Ludmila Alekseevna.' As if I've invited him. As if I need a guest in the house when I'm working. *V'gosti*. Ha! For a visit with your bottle, I can see."

Ludmila Alekseevna does not love Dyadya Gosha.

Pop picks up his soupspoon. "A quick *apertif*, that's all. Let the man have his small pleasures. He works hard. Just like you."

"Work!" she huffs. "Well, it's not for me to say what's work and what's not. Not for me to say how hard a black marketeer must work to bring home a sack of potatoes. Pretty hard, I suppose, if the man can't afford his own liter of vodka." She sniffs loudly, bangs the soup pot back onto the stove.

I catch her eye and stick out my tongue. She bursts out laughing. Ludmila Alekseevna does love me.

"Just turn the television on, would you?" my father says. "We'll watch the news."

"I'm watching *Youth Estrada* at eight," I remind him.

Ludmila Alekseevna covers the soup pot, turns the

gas on under the kettle, and then crosses to where the small black-and-white set sits under a large portrait of my mother on stage, her arms full of roses.

"So where's Ma?" I ask.

But before my father can answer, the static buzz from the television set gives way to an orchestral swell. It's Tchaikovsky. A familiar, grainy scene asserts itself from the fuzz. It's the Bolshoi Ballet's production of *Swan Lake*. It is 6:45 P.M. Moscow time on November 10, and in place of news, the First Channel is broadcasting *Swan Lake*. I look at Pop; he looks at me; Ludmila Alekseevna drops the teapot and covers her mouth. This is why— Tchaikovsky's ballet on the First Channel means one thing: real news. Not an update on the progress made in the North Siberian gas line, or a report on an honorary award given to some geezer in the Politburo, or a feature on the latest exhibit at the State Art Museum. *Swan Lake* means something significant. Something has happened in the Kremlin. And we will be watching old recordings of the Bolshoi until the Kremlin decides to let us know what.

"There she is," says my father in a strange, flat voice.

He nods at the screen, where Svetlana-as-Odette has entered the stage on the arm of her prince.

TWO
MUSSORGSKY

The next morning everything is changed. Officially.

I'm back at the table with Pop, drinking tea and eating jam straight from the jar, when they make the announcement:

"From the Central Committee of the Communist Party of the Soviet Union, it is with deep grief that we inform the Party and the Soviet People of the death of the General Secretary of the Communist Party and Chairman of the Supreme Council of the Union of Soviet Socialist Republics, Leonid Ilyich Brezhnev."

"There you have it," says Pop. "Eighteen years. Your whole life."

He is tired and he looks it. We had waited all night for what we suspected it might be—in part because you don't know a thing for sure until you do, and in part because we had forgotten that news from the Kremlin isn't the same thing as news from my mother.

Pop smoked cigarette after cigarette, Ludmila wrung her hands, and I watched the endless loop of weather forecasts that followed *Swan Lake* in the nonchalant programming that offered no clues except in and of themselves. There would be rain in Leningrad today, and it would be minus fifteen in Sivtikhtar . . .

"Oh, there will be blockades everywhere," Ludmila Alekseevna said, staring out the window onto the Ring Road. "And who knows what desperate things the hooligans in the street might get up to."

We urged her to stay the night, to keep vigil with us, but she only wrung her hands more. This is how simple Soviet people, the ones we call "Sovog," react to historic and tragic occasions—as if we didn't all know for the past five years that any day could be old man Brezhnev's last. Before long she was jabbering about terrorists and assassinations, so Pop trudged to the garage to get the car and drove Ludmila Alekseevna home.

He had told me to stay, "in case your mother calls." She didn't.

Now I glance out the window toward the Kremlin. The sun has been up for an hour but I can see that the floodlights are still on. I am waiting for a cue to talk about Ma. Pop, too, looks like he wants to say something. He begins talking about Shlosov and Krasin and other officials. "Andropov," he says. "Chernenko . . . Party Congress . . . We'll know soon enough."

It's strange to hear my father talk about politics in front of me, so I don't immediately realize that this (a subject normally off-limits) is somehow easier than talking about Sveta. It's hard to measure her absence, confused as it is with the bigger news from the Kremlin. Besides, she's left before. Flown off on a wild itch. Needing, she would say, solitude. Usually she went to the country, to the *dacha*, but sometimes she would stay at a friend's place. Years ago, before I was selected for the academy, she took a week-long vacation by herself.

"What about the spa on the Black Sea?" I hear myself suggest. "Remember the photos she brought back? How she said Crimea is the only place east of Cannes with proper sunlight?"

"Marya," he sighs. "Not even Danilov knows where she's gotten to."

This pisses me off. That he should state it so obviously.

"She could have run off with anyone," I snap. It is a nasty thing to say, but Pop doesn't seem to notice. Instead, his face goes slack. He turns back to the window.

"I don't think you understand. Your mother . . . She's gone."

"I *know!*"

Pop sighs and slips back into his bedroom. I listen hard and hear him pick up the telephone. He's rung a half dozen people since dawn, now that the lines are freeing up: friends, cousins, colleagues. What's he doing? Calling again to see if maybe they had been mistaken? That Sveta is actually taking a bath in their tub and they just hadn't noticed?

I start putting away the breakfast things. There will

be no school today. No repertoire. No rehearsal. I know this because Brezhnev wasn't the only sick old man running our country. In fact, he was so sick and old he really wasn't running things at all. The Motherland is in the hands of other sick old men. Two of them died over the summer, one after the other, and there was no rehearsal for two days. So I know that with Brezhnev—Secretary General of the Communist Party and Chairman of the Supreme Soviet—we've got at least a week of life-on-the-side.

In confirmation, the radio says the funeral will be held in five days. That "*Dear Leonid Ilyich*" will be laid to rest in the Kremlin wall along with the other "*great leaders whose continuation of the Revolution and of Vladimir Lenin's heroic founding of the first Socialist State has permitted us to shine as a glorious model for all the world's people oppressed by class warfare and capitalist inequality.*"

The announcer pauses.

Even on the phone in the bedroom, my father is silent.

The announcer continues: "All the People are invited to pay respects to our departed leader at the House of Soviets beginning on Saturday."

Ves narod: all the people. *Vsya jhizen*: all my life.

But all I can think is: What will I do next week, if life returns to normal and my mother is still gone?

The water from the tap has finally heated and it stings the cut on my palm. I wince and recall Dyadya Gosha last night rushing from the elevator:

"He's waiting for you," he'd said of my father. But

he had used the singular "you." In other words, he knew that my mother was not coming up, too. Which means that my father knew, even then, at just 6:30 P.M., that I was coming home alone. I turn the water off and sit down again at the table.

I'm an idiot. Pop knew she wasn't coming home last night.

"Pop." I holler. "Pop, come out here. Come out now."

I'm surprised at how quickly he's in the kitchen— turning up the radio, reaching for his cigarettes. "What? What are they saying?"

"Nothing," I answer. "I'm just thinking. You knew. You knew she wasn't coming home. So why don't you just tell me? Did you fight? Is she leaving you? Is that what you mean? *She's gone?*"

He lights the cigarette. I can't be sure, but I think his fingers are trembling more than usual. He opens his mouth, but I can tell that there is no truth waiting there. The doorbell rings. He closes his mouth and leaves the kitchen. I hear Dyadya Gosha's graveled voice.

"Throw roses on the corpse, my friend. It's the end of an era."

"Keep your mouth shut, you fucking goat," is my father's response.

HERE'S THE THING ABOUT Dyadya Gosha: He's a crook.

Pop always sugarcoated it. "He's an enabler. Open your eyes, Marya. You know what life is like for a girl who doesn't get fed from the currency shops? Whose mother has to cross half of Moscow to find decent boots for her kid? Whose Dad's salary hasn't changed since nineteen fifty-five even though he's got two babies and a car to fill? Yes. Gosha trades on the black market, and yes, the economic term for this is a 'speculator.' But take a look around at the state of things. Tell me that he's the one committing an economic crime against the people? Let Ludmila Alekseevna rail all she likes, but you know that three out of four pensioners wouldn't even have eggs without people like Gosha."

Mostly I believed him.

Gosha certainly wasn't a bad guy like on the cop shows. He wasn't hard and cruel, with tattoos spelling out his crimes across his hands and prison curses firing from his mouth like automatic weapons. The way I figured, he was like Robin Hood—if Robin Hood had to make a living, and there were no royal treasuries to rob and no Sherwood Forest to camp out in. If King John wasn't a gouty monarch and instead was just a make-believe economy, in which "we pretend to work, and you pretend to pay us."

But then two summers ago, I changed my mind about Uncle Robin Hood. That was the year that the Olympics came to Moscow. Virtually everyone we knew left for their *dachas*. There was no mass transportation except for the shuttles to and from the athlete's villages and the sports arenas, no meat except in the canteens for the foreigners, and there were roadblocks throughout the city and you couldn't walk in the center without a *militsiya* stopping you because you might be too drunk or too dirty to be seen as a model Socialist or, worse, you might be a spy on assignation with a Greek shot-putter. But Sveta had tickets to the closing ceremony, so we came back on the final weekend.

We found Georgi in our apartment, surrounded by enough Adidas sneakers to shoe half the Soviet Army, and some very dodgy assistants helping him take inventory. On further investigation we discovered an ugly hoodlum in the kitchen, his hands tied and one eye swollen shut in a purple bruise. He was babbling in Serbian, and one of Gosha's "assistants" was ignoring him as he counted out stacks of German deutschemarks. My mother went ballistic, raging at both Gosha and my father, who batted away her accusations with feeble entreaties. Then Gosha sent the goon squad away with the hapless Yugoslav and pulled out a case full of Hermes scarves and Bordeaux from under my mother's bed. My mother became appeased and then drunk.

From that day on I had no delusions about Gosha. He was both a crook and an enabler. Robin Hood and Mack the Knife. But he remained my Dyadya. This summer, when my mother was able to purchase five pairs of Levi's from the import shop just for the Bolshoi and give them to Gosha to sell for three times the price, Gosha grabbed her ass in both hands, kissed her heartily, and called her "Sveta, my angel, my guardian sister." He danced around the living room with her until she laughed and reminded him that he owed her a new TV. Instead, I got a new pair of leather boots for my seventeenth birthday.

Now Gosha and my father are whispering by the

door. It sounds as if they are talking about Pop's work, which is also unusual, since he works at a top-secret lab. I hear my father hiss *"Lukino"* as if it's a curse word and wonder again at the poison in his voice when Gosha first arrived. Caution, I guess. Brezhnev is dead, but you don't call him a corpse, nonetheless. Maybe Pop thinks his job is in jeopardy.

I dry the dishes and put the kettle on for another cup of tea. The radio is playing "The Volga Boatman"— funeral music. First Tchaikovsky and now Mussorgsky. Grim times.

"Marya, my sweet. What shall we do on this day of national mourning?" Gosha comes into the kitchen and ruffles my hair like I'm still a kid, then he picks up the cigarette that has been burning, neglected in the ashtray.

"Sleep," I answer, burying my head in my arms.

"Hear that, Vitya?" laughs Gosha. "Kids today. No sense of respect for their leaders. And probably equally ignorant about the opportunities that arise when those great leaders are dead. Vitya—you remember Stalin's funeral? How we larked about while *ves narod* was in a state of shock?"

Pop sits heavily in the chair next to me. "Things are different," he says. "Back then it was a real possibility— that the whole country might just wash up on the rocks without someone at the wheel. But today? Fifteen years now we're going pretty much nowhere. How can you worry about getting nowhere with no one at the helm. Anyway. It's all in order. There's stability in the Party."

I'm looking at Pop, listening to him say these dismissive

things, but I know he's nervous. His knee is jumping, and I can still see those frightened words (*you fucking goat!*) tormenting him like a persistent mosquito. But Gosha? He's as relaxed as the rabbit in the folktales.

"Marya, you wouldn't have believed what Moscow was like on that day—Stalin's funeral." Georgi pours himself some brewed tea, tops it off with hot water. "Every single citizen and the devil's own mother was out on the street. You've never seen so many long faces in your life. And I mean sober. Not a drop. You didn't dare. But your dad and I—we snuck off from the class. They made us go to the lying-in-state by schools, see, and our turn wasn't until three o'clock in the afternoon. So your dad and me, we tell the teacher that we've been selected by the Protocol Division of the Baumanskaya District Housing Association to collect the garland for Comrade Stalin's coffin. And that's what we did. With detours at a couple of other schools, where we enlisted the prettiest girls to join our delegation. Then we sat down by the canal and ate sweets until the damn bells gave us enough of a headache that we all went home. My God, how your mother laid into us when we came home, remember, Vitya?"

Pop tries on a thin smile. "Lots of people died that day. It could have been us."

I know he's talking about the stampede. The one that only recently got included in the official history. Hundreds of people were trampled to death trying to see Stalin's body as they carried it out of the Mausoleum. I remember how when I first heard the story, I couldn't believe it—mostly because by then we were taught that Stalin had manipulated his popularity, turning it into a "cult of personality" that did not reflect the true democratic spirit of the Soviet people. So this admission that the people, of their own free will, behaved so wantonly so . . . "cultishly"—it was something of an embarrassment. But the thing I really had trouble understanding was how Muscovites, having gotten through a terrible war (not to mention all the horrors of Stalin's so-called "revolutionary excesses") could still get emotional about death. If you were around in 1953, you had witnessed a lot of death. So why freak out about another one? Even his? Especially his.

Pop is right. There's no chance of that happening now. Our Soviet Union is nothing if not stable. Still, I can't help but wonder if it's fear on his face, and if it's there because our leader is dead and his wife is missing.

"Gosha," I say after a silence. "When did you last talk to Ma?"

The smile leaves his face. He glances at my father, but Pop is studiously grinding out his cigarette.

"Yesterday Ludmila Alekseevna told me that Sveta left early," he says, which does not answer the question. "She didn't take the car, she said. And she wasn't wearing her makeup." Gosha clears his throat. Gosha looks again at my father, nudges his elbow with his own. Pop doesn't look up.

"You're not talking?" he asks.

The silence seems endless. I'm looking from one to

the other, incredulous. They know something? They're keeping it a secret? From me?

Finally my father reaches over and grabs my hand. It's the hand that I cut and the more he squeezes the more it hurts. I'm surprised by the strength of his grip. He raises his eyes and I see they are filled with tears.

Oh, Pop. What have you been hiding?

"Marina. Your mother has been under a lot of stress," he begins. "She," he pauses, his mouth pawing for the words. "She has had more of her blackouts than usual. And she thinks there is a . . . a pattern."

Dyadya Gosha rises from the table. He turns the radio up louder; the Volga Boatmen are moaning their fool heads off. Then he goes to the fridge, pulls out a bottle, and pours a healthy slug of vodka, 100 grams, into a glass. He puts the glass in front of Pop. My father doesn't drink it.

"Your mother is afraid of something. But I don't want you to be afraid, Marya. There's nothing to be afraid of. But your mother . . ."

He's not making any sense. Who runs away because they are afraid? My mother is not afraid. She is nervous, yes. High-strung, yes. Sometimes irrational. Yes. These are things like having bunions and calloused toes. These are parts of being a prima ballerina. This is being Svetlana Dukovskaya.

Now it's Gosha's turn, and he's making even less sense.

"Marina—your mother thinks it would be better for all of you. In the West," he says. He's leaning into my ear, because even if he weren't a man who has engaged in illegal trade and "anti-state commerce," and even if he weren't in an apartment building known to be more closely monitored by KGB surveillance than most, you just do not say such things indoors in a speaking voice.

Shut your mouth, you fucking goat, I think.

He pulls a chair close so that his knee is touching mine. His hand is on my shoulder and his voice is in my ear. "Your mother needs time to think, *dochka*."

I want to stop him. I want to tell him I'm not his *dochka*, his daughter. But he's still talking, and I know that what he is saying is what my own father can't yet say. "There are many logistics to arrange. Many ways to accomplish these things, and your father doesn't agree with them all. Sveta's got one variant. You have another option. Your father a third. Now don't ask any more questions. Just give your folks time to sort this out. Maybe it won't even happen. Maybe everything will change overnight now— now that the political situation . . . But Marya, for God's sake. Don't ask. Don't worry and don't ask."

Then he downs the 100 grams.

I turn to my father, and he says something—something I can hardly make out from under the radio and Mussorgsky's much-too-loud brass. But I think what he has said is "end of an era."

ANYA CAN'T BELIEVE THE old geezer's dead. Can't believe the way everyone's acting like it's a tragedy. Can't believe we won't know if Winged Guitars won the *Estrada* prize for at least another week. Can't believe we get to attend the funeral with the entire Bolshoi company and upper management.

I don't say what I can and can't believe.

Pop and Gosha insisted that I get out of the apartment to "take my mind off things." But my mind is very stubborn. It stays in my kitchen where my father has equated today with the last day of everything I know.

"Marina, what's with you? You'd think someone died," Anya teases.

We're walking on the Arbat, one of the few streets where the population is allowed—in fact, encouraged—to congregate, to "express their shared loss" and "expound upon the virtues of our Party leaders." Sure enough, there's a small group of veterans and pensioners gathered at the bust of Lenin at the far end of the cobblestone street, listening to the proclamations of a young man who looks to be intolerably politically correct.

"Dear Comrades, today is a day when we reflect on the unwavering and bold progress made by legions of workers and steadfast followers of the word of Vladimir Lenin, the policies of the Communist Party, the guidance of the Supreme Soviet, and the valiant and bold leadership of Leonid Brezhnev, General Secretary of the Communist Party and Marshal of the Soviet Union. It is a day for you, dear Comrades and Party loyalists, to recommit yourselves to the love of labor and country that is your obligation as a happy and prosperous citizen of the Soviet Union. Continue taking part in the honorable task of building the brotherhood of the world proletariat and perfecting Communism."

There is a slightly larger group lined up outside the Kinotheater #14, where free ice cream is being dispensed along with black armbands.

"Look," says Anya, "the line's a bit shorter. Come on, it's ice cream, you ninny."

I follow her and we stand in line. She is yammering about her plan to stand near Aleck at the funeral and "fall all to pieces" on his shoulder.

"You know he has a girlfriend," I interrupt, needing something to say.

"Who? Yelena Ponamareva? That's over. She's sleeping with the guy they brought from Krasnodar. The long-haired one with the big, you know, Adam's apple."

"I heard Yelena likes big Adam's apples," I say, and Anya laughs too loudly.

She picks up news like a shortwave radio, Anya does. Sometimes I tease her that she knows what's happening before it happens. More and more, though, I think that it is me who knows what's coming. But at the moment I'm equally in the dark about what is happening, what will happen, and what has happened. For all my "visions," I'm now having trouble seeing what is right in front of me.

"So what do we do on Monday, for the funeral?" I ask.

"We're supposed to meet at the Bolshoi at seven A.M. Then they line us up, hand out wreaths, and we take our place on Red Square. After, we follow the procession up Gorky Street and back down to the Theater, where there will be some ceremony. Dasha says Vika says there's a short exhibitional something for such occasions. A *pas de deux* from *Giselle* or something somber—a requiem, basically." She pauses and looks at me, one eyebrow cocked. "Well, you should know, Marina. Hasn't your mother said anything? She would be the obvious candidate. I'm sure they'll have her onstage, even if she doesn't perform."

We've reached the front of the line. Anya's disappointed to find that there's only vanilla. She had hoped for pineapple or one of the other exotic flavors that our friendship with Cuba awarded us. I'm still fixated on her last words. Anya is right. Times like these are precisely why we have all these Artists of the People and Heroes of the Soviet Union, their chests covered in ribbons and medals and Orders of Lenin. They are important players in the propaganda machine. They have a very clear script to follow. But my mother is MIA. And if she is not back soon, Danilov will have a problem on his hands—there's no excuse for his cultural attaché to miss Brezhnev's funeral and memorial service. I wonder if he is making any more progress than my father in tracking her down.

Now Anya is tying the black band we were given along with our ice cream cups around her head, like a ninja. An old woman passes us and scolds us in a voice that sounds exactly like a goose. Anya quickly takes the band off and gives the old woman an elaborate bow. "A million words of gratitude for your kind remonstrance and moral guidance, Comrade Grandma," she says. I frown at her performance. The *babushka* is equally unappeased. "Shocking disrespect," she mutters. But I can see that the boys sitting on the heavy chain barrier on the side of the square are amused.

"Hey! Who are you, the wandering jiu-jitsu?" calls one, a joke that is either mildly anti-Semitic or a clever pun. Anya responds with a few steps of the *hora*, her arms waving like a rabbi, followed by a mock penitent act of crossing herself. All in all, a bold act on a crowded street full of watchful citizens "in mourning." Now the boys are impressed.

"Let's go talk to them," she whispers. And though my heart is not in it, I follow her lead and find myself flirting mindlessly with strangers on the Arbat late into the evening while Brezhnev lies in state and my mother lies in limbo.

Dyadya Gosha would be proud.

THREE
RIMSKY-KORSAKOV

On day two of our National Mourning, a man from the Ministry of Internal Affairs knocks on our door to tell us that Svetlana Dukovskaya has been institutionalized.

She was found, he says in mechanical phrases, on the grounds of a *zapretnaya zona*—a forbidden zone. She was shoeless and, worse, without identification. She was taken to the local police post where she became "delusional and aggressive." Her condition deteriorated overnight.

We don't ask which night that was.

"In keeping with protocol for the treatment of mentally compromised citizens, she was taken into custody by the State Psychiatric Directorate," the man says. "You will be given more information when it has been filed. I'm sure you understand that due to the heightened vigilance surrounding the current environment in the capital, and the associated need for calm in the provinces, the State organs are maintaining necessary caution over the dissemination of extraneous information. The Managing Soviet of Artistic Performers and the Governing Board of the Bolshoi Ballet have been properly informed. They will handle the associated dissemination of relevant information to the necessary recipients according to the established methodologies and timelines. There will be no announcement of this in the press organs until after the completion of the funereal events of the late Leonid Ilyich Brezhnev. Your duty as a citizen is to await further instructions."

The man, an overweight Party functionary with a small hole in his sock, writes down his departmental phone number and leaves.

No photographs fall from the walls. No broadcasts of *Swan Lake*, starring Svetlana Dukovskaya, interrupt the endless funeral dirge on the radio. There is no hint of our personal news blockade.

I am staring at my father in disbelief, because he is not on the phone. He's not calling any of the "connected" persons we know, sorting out what has happened to my mother and why. I suggest that he do this. He doesn't move. I watch his knee jumping uncontrollably. I ask him to talk to me. He is rubbing his thumb over his lower lip, lost in thought, but his eyes dart all over the room. I demand that he talk to me.

"Calm down, Marya," he says.

I call him a coward. I call him a deadbeat. I call him a parasite.

You know what a parasite is to a Russian? It is the worst possible creature. Worse than a speculator or a defector. It is someone who has taken advantage of the Party and the People to enrich himself with the fruits of our system.

You know what I think? I think my father knows that he is a parasite. He has known ever since my mother used her good name to get him a job at a top-level biochemistry laboratory at the Academy of Sciences. Because my father is neither an academician nor a biochemist. He's a simple chemical engineer from an undecorated family, whose only achievement beyond a diploma from a mediocre institute was in marrying a rising star.

"You owe her!" I shout, but even my shouting is programmed to be discreet. There is no question that the speech we just heard from the Ministry of Internal Affairs was written in advance of delivery. No question that the man who gave it had left us a fresh "bug" in our phone when he asked us to sit in the kitchen while he "packed a small bag for the patient." No question that the next visit and any information it contained would be partially determined by the conversation we are having now.

"Marya, get your coat," says my father through clenched teeth. "We are going out."

Down eight floors we descend with only the elevator's loud motor and the muted strains of Mussorgsky from every radio in the building breaking the unusual hush of a post-Brezhnev Friday morning. We cross the foyer, empty except for the twin concierges, who break their whispered conversation to watch us. For the first time, their X-ray stares worry me.

Outside we are greeted by an unseasonably warm gust off the river. It smells of algae and gasoline. We cross the road to the promenade on the embankment and walk in silence past a bench, where a man in a tan trench coat sits watching us from behind his newspaper full of nothing but the death of the General Secretary. When we are sure he is not following us, my father speaks.

"Do you know where the *zapretnaya zona* he spoke of is?" he asks. "It is Lukino, the laboratory where they implement the models from my department. Your mother has taken an interest in my work lately. I tried to avoid this, but she was . . . unreasonable."

All the world knows about the nuclear weapons that are at the root of our Cold War with the West. Nowadays this war is so cold it exists mostly in space or the hockey arena. But there's another arms race between us that fewer people know about, though if you remind them they'll say "ohIknowhowawfulhowdowesleepatnight." This is the race to create weapons not just of mass destruction—but of mass poisoning. Biochemical weapons. Germ weapons. Oh sure, they're doing it. In Siberia and in some Arizona desert and in all those black jungles and little islands where we fight our Cold War with soldiers who are used to the heat. And my father in his white lab coat is doing it, too—playing germ war. I know, for instance, the effects of botulism on bees. Of anthrax on ants. My father has told me about them—as a science lesson, of course. Not as a disclosure of state secrets. Pop doesn't know state secrets; he's just a low-level administrator. That's why he sleeps fine at night. Or, he did.

"Some time ago I came across documents," he says now, his voice below the wind. "Evidence that many years ago, there was an accidental contamination in the village outside Lukino. I can't tell how many people were affected. Probably the whole village, since, in fact, it doesn't exist anymore. The papers I discovered are not about the accident. They are about the cover-up. Extreme measures. Successful measures."

My father pauses, glances back over his shoulder. The man on the bench is nowhere to be seen. Pop takes my arm and leads me down the stairs that brings us to the water level. I'm surprised at the drifts of dead leaves. They have somehow defied the winds that make short work of autumn in Moscow.

"For many weeks, I did not tell your mother about this. It's not my place. And anyway it's over. Ancient history. If I should worry about my work, it's in other ways—ways in which we can repeat such mistakes. But then one day Sveta shows up at reception. Demands I come down. Tells me to leave for the day. She had had a . . . a vision. She told me she saw the results of this accident I'm telling you about. And the way it had been erased. Not cleanly, like a spill. But poorly, so that . . ."

He doesn't finish his thought. A ray of sunshine has broken through the overcast sky, landing on the massive façade of the *vysotka* that sits across the river from our own, like a comrade-in-intimidation for anyone enjoying a walk along the river. It's the Ministry of Internal Affairs. A chill runs through me. I thread my arm more snugly through Pop's.

"Is she sick?" I ask.

"She might be," he says quietly. "But worse: She knows something she should not. Something damaging. Something compromising. I don't know how. I didn't . . . I mean I don't know how. You know that she has a sort of sixth sense."

"What will they do?"

"That depends."

I wonder for a second if it depends on me. But it couldn't. This is a story about my mother and father. Not a story about their daughter. But that doesn't reassure me, because there shouldn't be any of those stories. It was my mother's decision (not my father's), at a crucial moment in her rise to the top, to have a child. She was just five years older than I am now when she refused, despite Pop's encouragement, to do what any other woman would have done—namely to get the first of her allocated five abortions. (Not literally. We're not China. Just a country short on condoms and long on "planned economies," even the household kind).

Just think, my joy, where I would have been without you? she used to say to me. *Never did I think I couldn't have it all. My ballet and my ballerina both. People know that about me. That I have it all. But only I know that without my daughter, I would have nothing.*

What had my father said that night, the night before she left? *Think of what you are asking.* What was she asking?

Why? Why would she throw away "it all" after she had defied everyone and struggled so hard? Why would she go bumbling into a forbidden zone? Why would she be barefoot? Why would she care about some stupid accident that had nothing to do with us? Nothing to gain for her daughter?

So I ask if maybe I misunderstood. "Pop, the other night, you were arguing. You said it was 'too soon' but she said it was time. What did she mean? Did she mean time for you to leave your job? Is that it?"

My father looks over his shoulder once more. He pulls me closer to the embankment wall and makes a show of adjusting the collar on my *dublonka*.

"No. She meant time to leave the Soviet Union. She wanted to escape."

The word is like an electric shock. Like the jolt up your spine when you land a jump poorly. Gosha was not making it up. My parents wanted to abandon the Motherland. And they were calling it "escape." Escape from what? Our luxury apartment? Our life of privilege? Our elite status in a less-than-elite society?

I'm having trouble breathing and my peripheral vision is going fuzzy. Again, the portrait of my mother, a shadow of her young self. My mother, aging in front of my eyes. Broken. Dashed. I see her now, barefoot on the wrong side of a chain link fence. I see her as an old woman, selling heads of garlic on a cardboard box. I can read a half-faded plaque behind her: LUKINO-13. I hear her say "*dochka*," my daughter. My knees are weak.

My father is tugging at me. "Keep walking, Marina," he says.

I brace myself against the railing between me and the river and breathe deeply.

"What did Gosha mean about different options?" I ask. "Was Ma going to go to America and stay?" I can't bring myself to speak the word. *Defect.*

"Georgi has good pull in the emigration office," he says. "He's been looking into the possibility of exit visas."

The Jew card. Pop wants to play the Jew card, the surest ticket out of the Soviet Union. The state has let tens of thousands out, second-class citizens with the stamp of *Yevrei* in indelible ink on their passports. Cause for insults, fines, and worse for decades. But now, because the Kremlin had to defend itself against a shrieking pack of "human rights watchers," that stigma was an invitation. If you are *Yevrei* in the Soviet Union in 1982, you've spent the last five years halfway out the door to New York, Tel Aviv, or Munich.

But here's the thing: Pop is the only Dukovsky with *Yevrei* in his passport. My mother is not Jewish, so neither am I. And in our house, on the eighth floor of the Krasnopresnya *vysotka* with a balcony facing the river and windows looking out on the Kremlin, no one has ever spoken of New York or Tel Aviv except as a stop on a two-week tour. My mother could defect. My father could emigrate as a Jew. Me . . .

I feel sick. *Sveta—it's time to think of Marina . . .*

"Keep walking," my father says again, grabbing my arm.

We climb back up to the street at the next stairway and turn toward Krasnopresnya. I catch a glimpse of the man from the bench at a kiosk across the street.

"Marina," says Pop. "You understand what is at stake here?"

I nod. But I don't. Not really.

"We have to keep cool for the next week. Mama is away at a sanatorium, got it? Exhaustion. Okay? When you go back to the academy next week, you have to play this role perfectly. Arkady Grigorievich . . ." He falls silent. The bench man is crossing to our side of the street. We say nothing until we reach our building.

A handful of passengers are getting off the tram in front of our entrance. Anya is among them. Pop stops and turns me to face him. I have never seen this fear in his eyes. This is not selfishness, not inconsideration— this is, maybe, survival.

"Not a stray word. Mama's at the sanatorium." He waits, anxious for my acknowledgement.

"Yeah, I got it," I say numbly.

"We'll get through this, you and me," he says.

He doesn't say, "you and me and Sveta."

IT'S STILL NOT ACCEPTABLE to gather at any of the cafés where we can play music or dance, so Anya suggests we meet Vika at Gorky Park.

"I've been calling all morning but no one picked up, so I just figured I'd stop by and get you," she says. "I mean, I don't know about you, but I can't stay inside another minute."

I can't either. I can't go into that den of paranoia. But I can't stand being outside either, where I have to pretend. The truth is I can hardly stand to be inside my skin. I look at Pop, and I see him tell me to play it cool. I kiss his cheek and say I'll be home for dinner.

Anya and I take the escalator down to the metro. The station is full of workers in brown smocks, polishing the marble floors, dusting the enormous chandeliers, removing the banners celebrating the Day of the Great October Revolution and replacing them with somber portraits of Brezhnev looking about twenty years younger than he is. Was. I feel that every one of them is on the lookout. For disorder, dirt, and would-be-defectors.

It's world-famous, our metro. Efficient, orderly, fast, and more elegant than any train station in Europe. That's because we're real proletariats. We choose mass transport as the rightful venue to be a "palace of the people." There's a lot of Moscow that looks the worse for wear, and even more that's flat-out broken. But the metro's not one of them. Anya and I wait for a train, surrounded by stained glass and tile mosaics and brass statues of partisans ready to ambush us from their marble pedestals. We are deep underground—deep enough to survive a nuclear strike if it happened today, as Ludmila Alekseevna fears. Several thousand citizens could take cover with us, and on weekdays at rush hour it feels like they are; but today, it's as quiet as the grave.

We take the train three stops and then cross the river on foot. The entrance to Gorky Park is shrouded in the same banners declaring the love of the people for the late

Leonid Ilyich Brezhnev. There's fresh paint on one of the columns, a shade lighter than the original. You can tell it's hiding an unofficial tribute left overnight. I think I can see the traces of "Lonya, we xxx you," but the message is fairly well obliterated.

Since it's a warm day the park is full of people who, like Anya and me, don't know what to do with themselves. The cafés and restaurants are still closed, but the liquor stores were open from noon until 3 P.M. It would be downright anti-Soviet to not provide a bottle for the family table tonight so that a toast can be made to the dearly departed. A quick look around confirms that many people aren't waiting until dinner. They sit on benches holding plastic cups, a telltale bag tucked behind their feet. Tipsy laughter punctuates the somber music warbling through the park's outdoor speakers.

Vika is waiting at the skating rink with two girls and a boy I don't know. She makes introductions and we stand around wondering where to go, since skating, apparently, has fallen on the unacceptable side of the "social amusements during National Mourning" division. Eventually, the boy, who's called Dima, suggests the boathouse.

Anya and the other girls forge the way down the hill to the lake. They all go to the same school and are talking about people I don't know. I fall back, lost in my thoughts. About halfway to the boathouse, Dima falls back, too.

"You're Svetlana Dukovskaya's daughter," he says. I

know he means it as an icebreaker, or maybe he's a fan. At any rate it's a harmless thing to say, normally. But things are not normal any more.

"That's right," I say, testy.

Dima just nods. We keep walking, listening to the girls' gossip without hearing what they are saying.

After a few minutes he says, "A friend of mine is Gagarin's grandson, and he says that every month he has to get tested for drugs."

"Drugs?" I ask. "Why?"

"Just, you know. You're held to a higher standard when you have a notable parent. Relative. Whatever."

"I guess so," I say, though why this kid thinks I have something in common with the grandson of the first guy in space is sort of beyond me. Is he asking if I have to get drug tested because my mother is famous?

"I guess you could say we've come a long way. I mean once upon a time, if your family was, you know, in the limelight . . . Well, the day would come when you would probably have to denounce your parents, like a good Pavlik Morozov." He pauses. "Or else go down with them."

I take a sideways look at this guy, who has decided that a good topic of conversation with a girl he doesn't even know is the story of Pavel Morozov—legendary boy hero and parent denouncer. Pavel sent his folks to the firing squad during the civil war because they hoarded some grain or something. Now he has a statue not far from my building, the treacherous little shit.

"But nowadays, they'd rather wash the dirty laundry than hang it out to dry."

This Dima, this standard-issue *botanik*—nerdy, and not in a cute way—is digging a very deep hole. I'm not a *komsomol* scout or anything, but I keep my distance from needlessly provocative talk like Dima's. I clear my throat, a warning.

"Or maybe," he continues, undaunted, "maybe they test him because someone actually wants the test to come out positive, you know? Because then they have something on Cosmonaut Gagarin. Something they can use."

I step in front of Dima and halt in my tracks. He nearly bumps into me, flushes red.

"I don't know what you're getting at, history scholar," I say in a low voice, "or why you think that this is a good time and place to let your mouth run off with your imagination. But it's got nothing to do with me, your thesis on family honor. It sounds to me like you have a buddy who got sent to fight in Afghanistan, got himself hooked on hashish, and is on track to sully his own good name. I'm guessing nobody really gives a shit about Gagarin's grandson, since space is about as exclusive as the bar at Kiev train station these days. As for Pavel Morozov, he was a rat bastard brat if you want to know my opinion. And I thank God we live in a time when the very term 'reactionary behavior' is a blast from a past that nobody remembers. Its meaning is clearly a mystery to simple minds like yours."

I stop.

Dima is looking at me with a queer half-smile on his face.

I am not keeping a low profile, I realize.

Up ahead the girls have turned to look at us. "Are you coming?" shouts Vika.

Dima and I apologize at the same time.

"I didn't mean anything," he stammers.

"Of course not," I say quickly.

Of course you wouldn't mean that I will either have to denounce my own mother or sacrifice my own name to save hers.

We hang out at the boathouse for about an hour, during which I keep far away from Dima. Then Vika slips and gets wet up to her knee, so we decide to head home. At the metro we part ways with Vika and her friends, and Anya and I are alone again on the platform.

"What's the story with that Dima guy?" I ask her.

She snickers. "Yeah, he's a weird one. But Vika says she has to hang out with him every now and then because he lives two floors down from her and his dad's in the KGB."

The Committee for State Security. The all-knowing, all-suspecting secret police. The KGB.

I'M LOOKING AT OLD photos and telling myself I have every right to hate my parents. My mother is a self-centered loose cannon and my father is a low-level parasite.

Here they are, at their wedding dinner. Sveta is laughing with her mouth wide open as Gosha makes a toast and a face beside her. She is so young and beautiful; he is so young and carefree. Between them is my father, with his unruly hair, his soft smile, and his oversized glasses. I can still recognize the man he was last month in this young groom. I can't recognize the man he is today.

Poor Pop. I know that he loves my mother. Loves her more than anything. I should be ashamed to call him a parasite. Anyway, it's inaccurate as a socioeconomic classification.

You can go to hell, Dima, I think. *I never called my father a parasite.*

All day long, day three of our National Mourning, my father has been sleepwalking. Scratching his head, which I swear has gone grey over night. "Going to meet Gosha," he keeps saying, "Gosha will be by soon."

Now Gosha is here. And I want to hate Gosha, too.

But do I?

I run my hand over the photo again. Three friends, all flawed, all frozen in time. Of course I love my mother. I love my father. But whatever love I have for Gosha is smothered right now. It's completely blocked by the understanding that I am desperately dependent on him.

Because this is what it means when your mother gets checked into a *durdom* crazy house in Russia when she's not, in fact, crazy: It means she has become a problem. And it means you are one, too. It means that if you want to bring her home from the *durdom*, you'll need to make sacrifices or pay a big bribe. This morning we ruled out bribery. Svetlana Dukovskaya has no price. Gosha won't say if they knew about her plans to defect.

"It's immaterial," he growls, angry at my father for

not understanding. "It's what she knows that is the problem. What she says she has 'seen.'"

The problem is my father and his top-secret job. The problem is that even if we decided to play "Mama's crazy so let's leave her in the crazy house with the rest of our tragic artists," there would still be a problem.

Pop pulls a cigarette from the crumpled pack on the table and says, "I'll play dumb." Neither Gosha nor I say he already is.

They move to the balcony as I flip through the photo album: Camping trips, New Year's Eve, a visit from Dad's grandparents—old-timers from the provinces who look like illustrations from a "Once there was a farmer" picture book. I turn the page, and I have arrived: a swaddled bug held aloft by my Pop; a red-faced blur in my peek-a-boo pram; a gap-toothed school girl with enormous bows for ears; and a first-year ballet student holding hands with Svetlana on stage at a People's Gala. The proudest daughter you've ever seen.

I close the album and think. Dima was right. Things have changed since the days of Pavel Morozov. Nobody is out hunting enemies of the people anymore. On the contrary, the mission is to hide the enemies before they can be outed. That's why we never hear another word about the defectors. That's why troubled characters vanish from history books, why they are erased from state records and newspapers.

If this Lukino business is really such dirty stuff and Sveta knows, there is no way she can be returned to her previous life and prestige. We can only hope that she can be returned silent and broken. But that can only happen if the Bolshoi gets itself a new Svetlana Dukovskaya—and quick; because for now, her absence is as problematic as her presence.

And I grasp at the only solution.

I step out on the balcony and say: "What if we could give them back the Svetlana they love? Would they surrender the Svetlana they don't?"

They don't get it yet.

"What if I could step into her shoes? Wouldn't that save the Dukovskaya name? Wouldn't it save Sveta?"

LATER THAT NIGHT, ARKADY Grigorievich Danilov calls to pass on his sincere condolences about Svetlana's "condition." The Party must have informed him that he would need a replacement for Brezhnev's memorial. My heart is racing as I lift the receiver of the second phone. The line is buzzing loudly, compliments of a KGB wiretap.

"We will all be thinking of her and looking forward to her speedy recovery," the director of the Bolshoi Ballet is saying to my father. I note that he has not said that he is looking forward to her speedy return.

Then he says that the Governing Board of the Ballet has recommended that official tribute to Svetlana be made "at a later date, when we are able to give her the attention and praise that she so deserves." My father must understand, suggests Arkady Grigorievich, that any discussion or mention of Svetlana even to speak of the eternal place she holds in the hearts of *ves narod*— not to mention the great esteem in which the Bolshoi holds her—would be premature, out of place, until the loss of Leonid Ilyich . . . at which point Pop says, "Yes. Of course. I understand."

But we all know that there is no such thing as an "eternal place" for a Soviet public personage—not in the hearts, minds, nor histories of *ves narod*. Especially if that personage has been sent to a psychiatric hospital. I know now that it won't be long before Danilov will be removing all the references to Svetlana Dukovskaya in the Bolshoi's printed materials. I know my father is thinking the same thing.

We've agreed that our best chance is if I take my mother's place on Monday and then (though I desperately want to think that Monday is enough to make everything okay) in the months that follow.

"And what are the arrangements for Monday?" Pop asks Arkady Grigorievich. "Where should Marina report for the funeral procession?"

There is a long silence. All we can hear is the loud buzz of the authorities listening, too. And beneath that, something else in the middle of the lapsed conversation—music. Ever so faintly, the famous melody of "The Flight of the Bumblebee"; Rimsky-Korsakov has apparently joined us on the line. For a moment I'm distracted by an absurd image of the great composer madly conducting the strings section of our Secret Police.

Arkady Grigorievich coughs. I wonder if he hears it, too, the misplaced music, or if it is only my anxiety. My fear of flight. The frantic tune generated in my own desperate head.

"Marina Viktorevna is excused from that obligation," he finally says. "We understand that she should be with you, her father, at this difficult time. And for the foreseeable future. Until, that is, her mother's condition stabilizes."

The strings in the background rise an octave. I open my clenched fist to find it covered in blood. The wound across my palm has opened. But beyond that, I see my own fate. Down the tunnel vision of my panic, I see in my hand a human heart. I squeeze it, my broken heart, and watch two drops of blood land on the carpet.

Now my father clears his throat. "You mean, Arkady Grigorievich, let me understand this. You mean Marina is dismissed from the company?"

I lift my eyes and try to focus on my father in the doorway of the kitchen, speaking into the other receiver. He is surrounded in a bright aura. I see only his silhouette as he places his hand on his chest. And again, on the floor before Pop, two drops of blood. My head is too light, and I slide to the ground, letting go of neither the phone nor the heart beating in my hand.

The line buzzes. The bumblebee grows more frantic.

"Surely, Arkady Grigorievich, this is unnecessary. Marina is the star of the academy, she is a critical member of the troupe, she should not, she cannot be dismissed so easily . . ."

But the director of the Bolshoi Ballet—reputed lover of my mother, mincing bastard and cheating sycophant—has hung up. The line goes dead, along with Rimsky-Korsakov's bumblebee and our only hope.

FOUR
WINGED GUITARS

It's just after 7 A.M., and all the bells in the city are tolling.

The title of that Hemingway book, what is it? *For Whom the Bell*? I remember how our English teacher would say, "Ford HOOM ze bell—indirect object." Of course I know for whom. But it feels like it's for me. I'm the indirect object.

Vera Petrovna is lining up her dancers to pay respects at Brezhnev's coffin; I am sitting on a suitcase just inside the threshold of my apartment. You always sit on your suitcase when you are about to depart on a trip. It is to ensure that you will return safely. I would be happy with a simple assurance that I will return at all. It is unlikely. The phone call from Danilov last night was followed almost immediately by a knock on the door. This time they took my father away for questioning.

By the time Dyadya Gosha arrived, I was hysterical.

He sat me down at the table, clicked on the radio, turned up the volume, and handed me two passports. The names were not ours, but the photographs were. He had tickets, too, in the strangers' names—leaving Moscow in seventeen hours, arriving in Simferopol on the Black Sea three hours later.

"There are no international flights," he explained, "because of the funeral. But my man in Greece has a small cargo passage from Simferopol in three days time."

We weren't playing the Jew card. We were playing from Dyadya Gosha's hand.

"Ma?" I asked.

"First you and Vitya," he said. He poured out a shot of vodka and drank it. Then he poured out another one and I drank it. The calm that came over me was not relief. Gosha led me out to the balcony. From across the river, the Ministry of Interior Affairs could see us but could not hear us.

I babbled questions, easier than accepting. "Why is this happening? You said that things might change. You said it was Sveta who wanted to leave. This is my mother being dramatic . . ."

Gosha answered without looking at me. "This is not just your mother. They have your father. But good. They'll let him go tonight. But I assure you; they will be back for him soon. As soon as they collect all the declarations and denouncements. They will be twisting these from the Academy of Sciences and from the Bolshoi. And then they will go after you. Lukino . . . it is bigger than just a sloppy job. It is one of our black holes. Your father is in it. You, Marya, are getting pulled in. Sveta . . . Sveta is already swallowed."

My father came home after four hours. He was gaunt, grey, nearly unrecognizable. His voice was gone. As though it had been removed. We sat in the kitchen, the passports and tickets in front of us. Pop found a piece of paper and a pen and wrote: *Svetlana told them more. Beyond Lukino. She knew more than even I know.*

"Is it accurate?" asked Gosha.

Too much to be made up. Details. Secrets.

My father lit a cigarette. His hands were shaking. His fingernails were bruised. He held the pen trembling over the paper and then wrote: *Human trials.*

Then he put the match to the paper, and we watched it burn. When it was nothing but ash, we started to plan.

IT'S EASY TO SAY that none of this makes sense and that it's somehow unbelievable. Because it is. But it's also true that it all makes perfect sense. I understand the system. Until now, I've never comprehended the terrible things it promises, only the rules it uses to do so. We have always followed those rules. Including today. The rules are: If you pose a problem for the Party, if you are a risk to the People, you must be dispensed with. So we are following the rules. We are dispensing of ourselves before the KGB can do it for us.

I understand.

And that leaves me sitting on my suitcase, which is hardly large enough to contain all my mother's scrapbooks, let alone my life. My father is on the balcony. Dyadya Gosha left around 4 A.M. Pop has spent the morning rehearsing the plan with me. Not for my sake though, I think. For his.

"She knew," he keeps saying. "She warned me."

Georgi reappears. It's clear that he hasn't slept, though he is clean-shaven and dressed. He takes one look at my suitcase and shakes his head, "Absolutely not." He hands me my dance bag. "This is all. "

I don't argue. I understand.

"Marina, Viktor Fyodorevich, chop chop," he says now, for the benefit of the bugs in the apartment. "Everyone is assembling. Let's go to the funeral." Pop, as practiced, says loudly, "I have a headache. I need to stay in bed. Take Marya with you."

In my bedroom I open the suitcase and remove just a few things, stuffing them into my dance bag. Pop is watching. He grabs me and holds me tightly against his chest. I can hear his heart beating. "Be brave, *dochka*," he says. "Be brave, my daughter."

I put on my *dublonka* and my beautiful boots, and I follow Gosha to the elevator and down eight floors. A light rain is falling as we hurry down the speckled sidewalk toward Krasnopresnya, where the *militsiya* are already corralling the people into orderly lines. My father, we have agreed, will follow us. We know that our building will be watched, but Gosha has a "guy" who will pull up behind Pop as soon as he emerges and hustle him into a dark black car. The car that will convince the watchful eyes that their own colleagues are following orders and that Viktor

Fyodorevich Dukovsky, associate engineer and administrative head of the Lukino lab, has been apprehended.

We are to meet at the small airfield south of the city at noon. Dyadya Gosha is confident that the speed with which we have committed ourselves to flight, coupled with the utter distraction of a State Funeral, is enough to ensure our escape.

"They can't possibly think that you will act so soon. And that shitty little airport will be manned by the nobodies today, when all the brass is on Red Square," he promised us.

Gosha and I descend into the metro with all the other good people of Moscow who are off to do their patriotic duty. We emerge with them, not far from the Bolshoi, then walk four blocks north and descend again. Gosha has planned our route, which takes two stations forward and one back, around and around the circular beast that is our municipal metro, until finally we find ourselves on a quiet platform far from the center. We exit, into a steadier rain, and walk through a deserted apartment block to a waiting car. Georgi grunts a greeting to the driver.

"*Poekhali.*" Let's go.

Gosha was right. There are just a handful of soldiers at the airfield. Miraculously, there is also a small prop plane standing on the tarmac. An old man in a fur hat with earflaps is fuelling it, a cigarette in his mouth. Inside the aerodrome there is a small waiting room; a café that appears to serve little more than popcorn, beer, and sausage; a heap of baggage carts with broken wheels; and a

single plexiglass booth into which every one of the officers on duty are packed. They are watching the funeral
on a small television. Mussorgsky has been abandoned
for Chopin's funeral march. The sonorous voice of the
announcer is naming the foreign dignitaries in atten-
dance, listing politboro members, noting the "plaintive
sky that cries with all the people on this day of great
sadness for the Soviet Union."

Ford HOOM ze bell tolls, I think.

Gosha directs me to a seat and raps on the door of the
booth. A man comes out, and Gosha speaks to him with
his back turned to me. The man looks at me over Gosha's
shoulder. He takes the passports that Gosha hands him
(*with what else?* I wonder) and retreats into another office,
this one behind closed doors.

There are only three other people in the waiting hall.
They are all men. One is old and carries a striped canvas
bag. One is Pop's age and carries a briefcase. The third
is a bit younger. His hands are in his pockets, and he
is sound asleep. I try not to make eye contact with the
other two.

An hour passes before my father enters the hallway.
I jump up, but Dyadya Gosha lays his hand on my side.
"Easy," he hisses. I walk nonchalantly to Pop and kiss
his cheek. We wait, watching the clock move in slow
motion and listening to monotonous exaltations from
the television. Every so often Pop leans over and asks
Gosha if he will . . . but before he can finish, Georgi
says, "Yes. Viktor, it will all work out."

Finally the officer emerges with our passports. He

doesn't look at us, just takes them into the booth. A moment later a pimply boy in an oversize lieutenant's hat calls out "Ivanov, Viktor Fyodorevich. Ivanova, Marina Viktorevna." His voice cracks on my name. For the first time I realize that Gosha has let me keep my Christian name.

My father and I stand. The boy beckons for us to proceed to the tarmac.

For one more second, we are a tight triangle. Of fear and fate. Then Dyadya Gosha takes a step back and says, "Okay, kids, have a good trip. No sunburns." He laughs at this hilarious joke, turns his back on us, and leaves. There is nothing as suspicious as a long goodbye.

And now we are racing down the runway, two of just eight passengers on this TU-143 if you include the captain, co-captain, and the sullen "onboard warden," whose job it is to yell at any passenger who lowers the blind or opens a thermos before we are airborne. We have liftoff. Out the window I watch the wooden roofs and tin garages of the suburbs recede. If I crane my neck, I can just see the cupolas of Moscow behind us. The heat from the engines casts a pall over the city, as if it's twilight. I close my eyes and see only darkness ahead, here at *the end of an era.*

Pop grabs my hand, the same one that I cut the night my mother failed to come home. It seems like so long ago. I wince, out of pain and terrible guilt. We are half-way to the Black Sea when I reach into my bag and pull out something that only my delirious state of mind could have made me think was vital to my escape. I slip a cassette into my black-market Walkman and press play.

Pereseki morya i okeany, no vremeni ni predavay, sings the lead singer of Winged Guitars.

Cross the oceans, but do not cross time. This is why I have left you behind. Vot tak, i vsyo.

PART TWO

BRIGHTON BEACH DECEMBER 1982

MUSIC FOR
A NEW YEAR

FIVE
TATTOO YOU

It's been more than a month since they put Brezhnev in his grave, and I'm watching them do it all over again.

I'm in a flannel nightgown 5,000 miles from home, but I'm looking down with a bird's eye view at the geometric study in grey that is Red Square during a State Funeral: marching rectangles of great-coated soldiers and gloved sailors; motionless squares of regional bosses and Party apparatchiks; a perimeter of stolid men and women bearing larger-than-life portraits of the dead man and, occasionally, dabbing away invisible tears. Now into the square rolls a grey-green tank, the torso of a saluting officer springing from its head like Athena. It is conveying a blood-red coffin in which Leonid Brezhnev lies like an overfed vampire.

My English is not strong enough to follow what they are saying on this American television. Not without concentrating, which I have difficulty doing. I hear the

name "Andropov" with the accent on the wrong sylla-
ble. That's the name of the new old guy who is in charge
at the Kremlin, but looking at them all lined up on the
tribunal—tiny figures against the meat-colored marble
of the mausoleum, some wearing fedoras and some
wearing fur *shlyapas*—I can't tell one from the other. It
must be this guy who has stepped up to the microphone
to promise that the "Global Communist Movement will
continue and triumph." He must be our new leader, Yuri
Andropov. The others look like they are wondering if
smoked sturgeon will be served at the banquet afterward.

Why am I watching this predictable display again?

Believe me, it's not because I want to relive that day.
These are the same images I glimpsed in black-and-white
from behind the Plexiglas window in the airport that
could have been my prison. These are the images that
flickered at the edge of our consciousness, me and Pop,
as we watched Dyadya Gosha stroll out of the airport
with his hands stuffed in his pockets and not a single
backward glance. I know exactly what's coming. Down
goes the coffin and 3,000 armed soldiers raise their rifles
in salute. The Kremlin bells groan, sonorously, and
soon all of Moscow joins the final farewell to Comrade
Brezhnev. And I am boarding a plane for the Crimea.

I have no memory of the hours that we spent in a
small, off-season hotel room in Simferopol waiting for
Gosha's Greek to contact us and smuggle us onto his
small vessel.

I don't remember the things I said to my father as we

rocked across the Black Sea, which I had never known as anything other than sparkling blue and about six feet deep. (That's if you are swimming distance from the tanned, oiled lifeguards and the cold apricot juice sold by the cripple with the cart on the boardwalk. But the Black Sea is black when you are far from shore. It's a very wide sea indeed if you are contraband and en route to the West for the first time ever under a very dark cloud.)

I don't even really remember Greece, my first taste of the West. I was sick when we arrived in Athens. Pop found medical help until my fever went down. *She's improving*, I kept hearing, in my delirium. I had hoped that I was overhearing a conversation about my mother. By the time I was well, my father had secured everything we needed to continue. On November 30, 1982, we arrived at John F. Kennedy airport in New York.

That was three weeks ago. Every day since then I have listened to the planes overhead coming in for landing. I've wondered what their stories are, the people who are joining me in exile.

Why am I watching this program, an "expert investigation" called *Inside the Kremlin Today* that shows me nothing but the Kremlin yesterday? Maybe I think that this time I'll catch a glimpse of Vera Petrovna and my dancers. Maybe I'll see Anya, crying on Aleck's shoulder, and I can wave goodbye. Maybe if I watch it until the end, the American will tell me what happens next. Will show me pictures of Moscow after the funeral. Will tell me whether people still go to the ballet, still study for exams, still fall asleep at work, still put jars of pickled garlic on the balcony for winter. But he doesn't know. He doesn't even think to wonder, as I do, whether Winged Guitars won *Youth Estrada*. Whether my mother is delirious or getting better, and whether Gosha is there to hold her hand. The man talking on the television is only wondering what will happen between the United States and the Soviet Union now that Brezhnev has been interred.

I want to know what will happen between the United States and the Soviet Union now that they hold joint custody over my life.

I get up from the couch and turn off the television. I am standing in a room half the size of my old bedroom. There's a sofa that is no more than a mattress on a frame and a round table covered in oilcloth. Pop brought home a portable tape player with speakers last week, so we have music as well as television. "Boom box," he'd said, his accent celebrating the percussive nature of the thing.

I press PLAY. The music doesn't really boom. It envelops me like a blanket that I want to pull over my head. I have spent many days hiding under the songs of Winged Guitars.

This is where I live now. In a small apartment above a shopping strip on the southernmost tier of Brooklyn, New York. Behind this building are a wide wooden boardwalk, a stretch of dirty sand, and the Atlantic Ocean. Outside the front door is an elevated train. The Q train. We don't even have such a letter in Russian. But the Q train dead ends in Brighton Beach, also known as

"Little Odessa" or "Russia by the Sea." About half a mile west of us America begins, speaking English, Spanish, and slang. But here in Brighton Beach you mostly hear Russian. We live in a Soviet-exile ghetto.

Every day, Pop climbs up and down stairs along Brighton Beach Avenue, inquiring, registering, applying. Twice he has placed phone calls to Moscow, to numbers that Georgi supplied before we left. But they have gone unanswered. Once he took a risk and called the hospital where Svetlana was taken. Somehow he managed to persuade the operator that he was calling from East Germany "on business." She told him that my mother had been transferred but that he would have to inquire further with the Ministry of Health on his return to Moscow. I was merciless that night. I called my father a traitor and a backstabber and a helpless jackass. He went out and drank too much.

But here's the thing: I've never climbed the stairs along Brighton Beach Avenue, let alone board the Q train to see what it was my mother had hoped to bring us to. I haven't inquired or registered or made phone calls, though my English is better than Pop's. In America, school is out for Christmas vacation and won't start again until after the New Year. But I'm not looking forward to that, either—making friends, testing my English, explaining myself. So what do I do? Nothing. I wrap myself up in my music. If I leave the apartment it's only to brood on the boardwalk or walk the main drag with the *babushki* inspecting the parsley, the hairstylists in leopard prints singing Alla Pugacheva, the street toughs smoking Soviet *papirosi* without the filters. If I liked vodka more I would drink too much, too.

The phone rings, and I know it's Pop. There's no one else it could be. No one knows who we are. No one knows we are here. His voice is unexpectedly chipper.

"Marya, Maruska-Papuska," he gurgles. "How are you?"

"Fine," I say, worming my finger through the curly tunnel of the phone cord.

"Slept late?"

"Hmmmm."

There's a lull. Pop wanting to fill it.

"We have an invitation for New Year's," he says. "A former colleague. Well, a colleague of a colleague. You don't know him. He was at the Academy when I was still at the Institute. In short, I made contact. He's been here eleven years, Marya, and knows his way around. He's going to be a huge connection, *dochka*, huge. And he has a son your age."

"That's good, Pop." My father's speech has become peppered with the phrase *in short*. We avoid lengthy discussion.

"So it will be a nice party, Marya. And we will have people, you know? We have to start meeting people. Building a—an American life." Pop's voice dies under the screech of a fire engine.

I wait for the siren to warp past and ask, "Did you call Georgi? Have you heard anything . . ." but the racket is back, drowning my voice on his end. In America they respond to emergencies loudly, not like at home where things are taken care of with shushed mouths.

"Marya," he says when the second wave of sirens passes. "I don't have another quarter. But go buy yourself a dress for the party, okay? There are some dollars in the kitchen drawer. With the spoons."

"Sure, Pop," I say. He never uses the word *money*. Money means *dollars*.

I go into the windowless and narrow kitchen. We have a dozen plastic cups, some chipped china from the Good Will store, and a refrigerator full of beet salad. Also, $145 in the drawer with the spoons. I know that this is more than I need for a dress, because the prices on Brighton Beach Avenue are as cheap as the merchandise—all the sales ladies and half the dresses look like they'd be more at home in Snooze-o-grad, Russia, than at Bloomingdale's. But I'm also pretty sure $145 won't pay the rent next month, and I don't know if Pop has more, where he could get it, or even where he got the dollars that are here now.

Last night he was circling jobs in the paper. Lab assistant, retail salesman, junior pharmacist.

In short, we're living on our last kopecks. Maybe this "huge connection" will bail us out.

I pour myself a glass of juice, close the refrigerator, and follow the hallway farther down the tracks of this thing they call a "railroad apartment" to my closed bedroom door. Pop had insisted that I take the bedroom, and I didn't argue, because it's the only place in the apartment with sunlight. That's why I keep the door closed. Like I'm hoarding the sunshine. When I see the sparkling water outside my bedroom I feel the smallest bit of relief. Like I won't, in fact, suffocate after all.

It doesn't seem fair, does it, that I should feel like I can't breathe because I have escaped?

I undress, shower, and then I put the nightgown back on. I take my time combing conditioner into my hair, painting my toenails, eating the last of the canned peaches, and rewinding the tape of Winged Guitars again and again and again.

It's nearly two o'clock. I wonder how to fill the remaining six hours before Pop arrives home. He is trying harder than I am to make this new life work, but he gets confused from one day to the next about how to do that. He believes that the KGB will find us here in Brighton if we take back our identities as a low-level official at Lukino and a junior ballerina, husband and daughter of the debilitated and disgraced Svetlana Dukovskaya. Anyway, those identities are gone, left in the *vysotka* on Krasnopresnya along with everything else. We are not Dukovskys any more. We are Ivanovs. "Joe Blows" as they say in America. Joe Blow-skis. When he's feeling optimistic Pop says, "Marya, don't you know that is what America is for? It is for reinventing yourself. You go in as a *shtetl* peasant or a disgraced aristocrat or a moonshine peddler, and you shed it like a cocoon. You emerge a Rockefeller. An Einstein. Elton John!"

I don't tell him Elton John is British. Or that he always has been. That his cocoon was a strange den of drugs and decadence that would scare the shit out of a good Soviet like my father. And I don't need to tell him the less optimistic interpretation, that all "we" are is a terrified pair who owe everything to a woman whose name must not be named if we are going to reinvent ourselves.

I pour myself another glass of juice but don't drink it. It stands abandoned on the kitchen counter while I pace, wondering if this "colleague" could really do something for us. Solve this conundrum in which we aren't who we were, but aren't who we are.

My toenails have dried, and I put in another cassette. I know I need to stop listening to Russian music like it's life support, so I put in *Tattoo You* by the Rolling Stones. The first song starts with a lone guitar riff, followed by a drumbeat that is pure adrenaline. Hot blood. Powerful Lethe. Serious dance music.

Start me up . . .

On an impulse I pull my dance bag from the shelf in the closet where it has been lying since we moved in and lace my shoes on. They feel wonderful. They feel hard like rock music and pliant like a drum skin. They feel sexy, like Mick Jagger. I am started up.

I haven't danced in a month and now I do, in a full rejection of classical choreography and Bolshoi standards. I pull off this nightgown that has become my shroud and dance in my bra, panties, and toe shoes. For the first time in a month, I feel alive, leaping down the corridor, scattering the lethargy of these restless days. I whip my head and my hair is electric. I abandon my arms to their own wild *port a bras* and I land a triple pirouette with one foot on a kitchen chair, riding it to the ground like it's a junior dancer from Krasnodar.

I can almost hear Vera Petrovna now: "Marina! What is this emotion? Can you not control your movements?"

I can. But I will not. Not today.

The boom box is on top volume and there is a pounding on the door. I unlock it and open it just a crack to the downstairs neighbor, Sonya Moiseevna, wide-eyed in her housedress.

"*Gospodi bozhe moy*—I thought the ceiling was coming down, but it's just you, *devushka*, bless you. Turn down that dreadful rock and roll and behave yourself."

I apologize and close the door behind her waddling frame. Then I make a decision. Marina Ivanova, whoever she is and whoever she isn't, must be a dancer.

THE Q TRAIN IS waiting on the platform, the end of the line. I've watched it pass the apartment on its elevated tracks three dozen times a day for the three weeks. But here, at rest, it is a different beast all together.

It stands shuddering and waiting and suddenly exhales all its doors open as if it had been holding its breath. It's ten cars long and its paint has peeled—splotchy, like a burn victim. Adding to its general disfigurement, it is defiled with graffiti: indecipherable messages disguised in the bubbled and rounded script of cartoons.

I'm accustomed enough to the western alphabet. Its characters are individual and assertive. And they are used by assertive individuals, these Americans who prefer bold block letters over the refined flow of cursive. I can read the street signs in these letters, and the television guide and advertisements: CALL NOW. JUST $7.99. NO SWIMMING. But this graffiti on the train, and on the far wall of the handball court, and on the delivery trucks outside the grocery store—these strange twentieth-century hieroglyphics seem to convey something sinister.

On the dinged-up flanks of the car before me, I make out the letters *RSTA-BloDog!* With the exclamation point, it strikes me as something I should respond to.

"Tattoo You," I whisper.

I've heard something like that down at the hard icy field where the boys from west of Brighton gather to taunt each other from their too-small bikes. *What, you don't like my face? Tattoo You!*

The train takes the steep curve at Coney Island Avenue and heads north. We are above ground, surveying a landscape of water towers, cemeteries, and postage stamp yards adorned with laundry. I can see the ocean that I have left at my bedroom, my exiled countrymen strolling unhurriedly across the boardwalk.

Farther down the beach I can see the spire of the Coney Island amusement park—a strange landmark that looks like the rusty result of Soviet construction and Eiffel Tower copycats, topped with a tea strainer. I walked down last week. It was a cold afternoon, late in the day, clouds overhead like shifting bruises. I sat there with my depression, shut up and shut down as the gates on all of the funhouses. But today the sun is bright, and the track has straightened out, and I have the Rolling Stones in my ears as I watch the rails ahead.

On either side, apartment buildings line the tracks so closely that I can sometimes see into people's lives as they change their clothes, wash their dishes, switch the dial on the television. At every stop, more people board the train. Old women, young men, mothers with babies. Across the subway car, two teenagers in leather jackets and fingerless gloves are cutting their eyes at me. They speak to each other in loud voices, but I don't understand them. They might be speaking graffiti. I think one says to the other "RSTA Blo," and the other one says "yo." They get off at the next stop. I cut my eyes at them as the train pulls out, but they have already forgotten me. *Tattoo You.*

Manhattan is not something we've really discussed, me and Pop. If you tracked the past weeks of his busyness and my brooding you would have a harmless funnel cloud over Brooklyn, touching down on Brighton Beach Avenue and the boardwalk, rustling the trees along Ocean Parkway, and jerking only as far north as the courthouses and social services buildings in downtown Brooklyn.

If Pop has taken the train into Manhattan, I haven't heard about it. Manhattan is about as relevant to us just now as Hollywood or Siberia. Except those are places where in alternate realities I might have found my mother. For about the hundredth time, I wonder if my mother is languishing in a hospital in Siberia. Or doing manual labor in a camp in Siberia. Or organizing a ballet school in some closed city in Siberia.

I flip the tape in my Walkman to Side B and rise to

stand at the front of the car where a window gives me an unobstructed view of our destination. We are climbing a steep grade, and at the top I can see a skyline on the horizon as shocking and impossible as the Emerald City of Oz. It actually sparkles. It's all glass and steel and water, dancing in the sunshine, and for the first time in far too long I feel something familiar. It's like the stage lights have gone on and illuminated a new backdrop. Without even trying I can see myself in the spotlight.

Then the subway train descends underground, and my confidence disappears as quickly as the glittering city.

Now, as the train trundles under water, losing speed and sounding its horn, I just hope that the first thing I will see at the next station are those assertive letters L-I-N-C-O-L-N to point me in the right direction, because the subway map, covered in its graffiti tattoos, does not. I turn off the music in my ears. I need to concentrate.

Lincoln Center is where American Ballet Theatre is. The best ballet in America. And if it keeps stealing all the best Russian ballerinas—the best ballet in the world. But no. Not yet. The Bolshoi is still the greatest.

If things had gone differently, I would be going to Lincoln Center with my mother as my introduction. She would have waltzed into the American Ballet Theatre and ushered me into the Artistic Director's office where Baryshnikov himself would have greeted us. The idea gives me goosebumps. Mikhail Baryshnikov. Our greatest dancer. Our greatest traitor. He defected four years ago. I hadn't forgiven him. But now I could imagine him saying to me, *Pleased to meet you Marina. Let's see how much of your mother there is in you.* And then Sveta would buy me legwarmers like the ones she brought back once from a tour. Legwarmers with *ABT* up the side, and we would have had lunch at the café across from Lincoln Center. The one with the green salads and the fresh squeezed fruit juice and the tables on the sidewalk. Sveta had shown me the pictures.

Of course, that would have been only if things had gone differently, and then gone differently again.

What if things had just never gone differently in the first place? If nothing had forced me to change my name, forced Pop to start all over; if my mother had stayed the Soviet Union's most vibrant cultural star, instead of being dead to it. Or just plain dead. She could be, I know. They have powerful medicines in our psychiatric hospitals.

At Pennsylvania Station, I get off the train. The station here is big, like the hub stations in Moscow. It is also filthy, crowded, and shameful. Yes, that's the word I would use: shameful. The ground is littered with trash and with bums, men with dirty clothes and long beards and carts full of more trash. In Moscow these men would be in the *durdom*, without question, or at least in the sobriety cell with the worst of our *alkashi* drunks.

The walls of the station are grey tiles, like at the shabby water sports complex in the factory neighborhoods of Moscow. The ceilings are low and echo with the constant din of people shouting, crying, running in their shiny shoes. I head for an EXIT sign, only to find it barred with giant turnstiles and an endless stream of passengers. There is another exit further down the passage but a phalanx of police officers—fat, blue, hands on hips—makes me turn back.

I'm beginning to sweat in the underground heat. I'm accosted: first by a woman with a map, a suitcase, and a baby in a stroller ("I don't know, I don't know," I say); then by a tall man with a fist full of money and another hopeless request ("I don't know, sorry," I say); and then by a group of energetic black boys spinning on their shoulders.

Eventually I find my way out in a narrow stairway that smells of urine. But in the open air I discover the same shameful disorder. Traffic is backed up, faces are twisted, garbage darts across the street like stray cats. Dirty snow piles up between cars and melts in grey puddles in the gutters. I see more street dancers, hear more boom boxes. People who look more male than female flip their skirts in the crosswalks. Food carts, newspaper vendors, and loud men with crosses around their necks have turned the sidewalk into an obstacle course. There is a rat feasting on what appears to be a chicken leg. It's as if Oz turned out to be the Inferno.

Above me the buildings no longer sparkle. They glow with the purple and green of neon, struggling against the daylight. Beyond these electric façades the buildings form dingy yellow canyons of elevator banks, boarded windows, and untethered banners advertising parking rates. Directly in front of me a taxicab screeches its brakes and a skinny figure does a backflip over its hood. The cab driver is out on the street in an instant, yelling fast and loud. The skinny figure jumps up and flashes a toothy gin. "Yo," he says, followed by more rapid-fire graffiti-ease.

It seems impossible that there should be a piano somewhere near running scales through the *tendus* and battements of a warm-up. But I realize that this what I should expect from now on: the impossible.

"Lincoln Tsenter," I whisper several times, and then I ask the man selling hot dogs from his cart. "Where is Lincoln Tsenter?"

He points and I walk that way. After several more blocks I ask again and a man gestures to the left with his rolled up newspaper. I plod on, the wind whipping my hair, the noise of the street a constant harassment. There are fewer people walking with me now, and soon I have to stop. Before me is the river. At my back, the *whoop whoop* of Manhattan, but I can feel it sneaking up on me. I haven't left it behind.

Here's a storefront window hung in shabby red curtains. Its awning promises DANCING GIRLS. This is not, I know, the American Ballet Theatre.

Across the street, above a pizza parlor, a woman with a sparkling sweatband around her forehead opens a window, letting out music and shouting. "And One and Two and Three and Four . . . Kick, bring it up, bring it down, and punch it out! And One and Two and Three and Four . . . Five more sets of kicks and work it ladies, love it!!" Behind her I can see the bouncing heads of many other women. Who knows what the bottom portions of their bodies are doing. This, too, is not the American Ballet Theatre.

A bus pulls up alongside me, opening its doors so that I can see the driver as he announces, "Port Authority. Last stop."

I watch them file out, these New Yorkers who seem not to notice anything other than the space between them and the person in front of them. When they have all disembarked and fanned out across the street, I call up at the bus driver: "Excuse me. Please tell me where is Lincoln . . ."

He interrupts me. "That's it right there. Lincoln Tunnel."

I look to the four lanes of traffic. At the policemen blowing their whistles, waving their arms, corralling the cars speckled with salt and snow and grime into a congested, impatient exit from the city. I'm gazing into the dark maw of a tunnel to I don't know where.

This is worse than arriving at ABT as a nobody, I think. This is a metaphor for just how blind I am in my new life.

THAT NIGHT POP COMES home to an empty apartment. He puts water on to boil and pours himself a drink. That night I come home to an apartment where my father is making macaroni in his undershirt. He hugs me, and I smell vodka on his breath. I ask for a drink, too.

That night Pop and I talk.

We talk about Manhattan and I tell him about my pilgrimage to Lincoln Center that ended at the mouth of a tunnel. I tell him about the dozens of dance halls to be found there, pulling the stack of postcards from the pocket of my coat and spreading them out on the table: *Sweet Dreams, Exotic Dancers, Adults Only, Dusky Dancers, Midnight Riders*.

"Oy, Marya," says Pop. "Don't give me heart attack."

But he is laughing, because I am, too. It's funny, after all. I had gone all the way to Manhattan. I had planned to take the city by storm. Instead I found its messy underbelly and an exit hole. But I recovered from the shock, inserted headphones in my ears, spun on my heels, and bought myself another Rolling Stones cassette. And a fifteen-dollar party dress. I rode the Q train home in small triumph.

After dinner I model my new dress for Pop. Sapphire blue, a ruffled elastic band made to expose the shoulders. A satin sash across the waist. I share with him the words I learned that day: "aerobics," "jazzercise," "remainder," "for handicapped," and "two for one."

I tell him how astonishing Filene's is, the store where I found the dress. How there were two full floors with racks and racks of clothes. How many different people were looking for clothes—young, old, black, Chinese, fat, really super fat. How there was a woman who must have been a movie star in her enormous sunglasses and fringed jacket and shiny gold blouse cut down to below her cleavage. She had gold highlights in her hair, too, and green eye shadow when she took off the sunglasses. She had been flipping through the hangers next to me when I pulled out the blue dress. She took it from me, held it to my chest, and said, "Oh yes. Absolutely. Stunning. Very girl-next-door, too. That's the one." Then she had handed it back to me and disappeared.

He pours me another shot, and when I have drunk, I put the Rolling Stones on the boom box and laugh as Pop demonstrates his own style. "Very funky white boy," he says in English, waggling his eyebrows. Pop's been listening to the radio.

Later we take a walk on the boardwalk. We breathe in the sea air that seems as far from Manhattan as it is from Moscow. I wrap my arm around Pop's waist, and I say, "Ma will be happy here."

I don't even mean it. I mean, I don't really believe it. The "railroad" apartment, even with its seaside location, will never make Svetlana Dukovskaya happy. Sveta would not be happy with our slightly drunk dinner of macaroni, or even my $15 discount dress. Certainly not the American craze for aerobics. What I meant to say is that Sveta would be happy rearranging America to suit us. She would be happy lifting us by the scruff of our necks from Brighton Beach and installing us in a glassy skyscraper far above the horns of the Lincoln Tunnel.

But it doesn't matter what I meant. Because my father hears me say, "Ma will be happy here" and he doesn't care about happy or not, he only cares about that future tense. *Ma will be here.*

"I hope so, *dochka*," he says, squeezing me back. "I will do anything to bring her. Anything and everything." It's more determination than I've heard in him since we left home. We walk a bit farther in silence, listening to the distant surf. Then Pop starts talking.

"Your mother had a gift," he says. "Like many gifts, this one was a curse. I don't mean her talent as a dancer. I mean the way she saw things." He pulls a cigarette from his pack and struggles to light it in the strong sea breeze. "It began some time ago. We would be somewhere—in a historic place—maybe one of the palaces outside Leningrad, and she would recount for me the events that had taken place there. She was so detailed. So specific. And she was always accurate in the dates and the people and the significance, just as we are taught from the histories. But she would also describe things that were never documented. Disturbing things sometimes, or sometimes . . . just interesting. Real, you know, like they were so vivid that you just knew it was true. Once at Danilovsky, she saw wild dogs with the bones from a mass grave. When we swam at the Chaika, she whispered to me, 'The archbishop swallowed poison on the day his wife died, but the chapel keeper, just an orphan from Tver who had no parents but the church, found him here at the altar. The boy forced him to drink kefir until he vomited up the poison. He lived to be eighty-four and died of a heart attack in his garden.'"

We are at the end of the boardwalk. Beyond are unfamiliar neighborhoods, more water, the airport, and then *terra incognita*.

"I thought: what on earth?" Pop continued. "But she was seeing a scene from the Cathedral that stood for thousands of years on that embankment, until Stalin blew it up and put a swimming pool in its place. In short, Sveta could see the past."

I sit down on a nearby bench and put my hands in my pockets. *Sveta could see the past*. He is using the past tense. *Sveta will like it here.* I am using the future tense. There is no present tense. This is important.

"I have it, too, Pop," I say finally. "I see things other people don't."

My father stands still, looking out to sea. He says nothing, as if he hasn't heard me.

"I think we both suffered more than we knew back home," I continue. "Maybe physical strain or emotional stress. We'll be better here. At least there's that."

I want to believe it. It could be true. I haven't had a single episode since we left. So that must be it. That's why our escape was necessary. And now we can rescue Sveta. We will spring her from the KGB and save her from her visions at the same time.

I glance at my father; his laugh lines are gone. He has aged years in the past month. How will he bring Sveta here? How will he rescue her? He's not even reacting to my words. I could tell him about how I saw Sveta grow old when she was banished from the portrait wall. I could tell him how I saw him on the phone, pleading, his chest a giant mortal wound.

Suddenly I have a terrible headache, maybe from the vodka. Pop lights another cigarette, but I pluck it from his lips and grind it under my heel.

"C'mon Pop. Let's go to bed," I say, in short.

SIX
SONGS IN THE KEY OF LIFE

It's New Year's Eve. *Novi God*.

Outside my bedroom window the sea is gone, hidden behind a white curtain of snow. Inside, with all the lights off, I can see my reflection, doubled in the two darkened windows.

I would like to appear at the party precisely as I see myself in the unlit theater of my windowpane. Silent, graceful, but ultimately not there. Just a silhouette, a sylph—a ghost on a silent stage. That would be best. I wouldn't be approached, asked, engaged. And I wouldn't have to worry that my off-the-shoulder dress is a giddy thing to wear out in a snowstorm. All sylphs expose their bare shoulders. I watch my double-self gather a slow *developeè*, stretch into long *arabesque*, wrist flexed lightly, like the tip of a seabird's wing. The ruffled skirt of my dress falls prettily.

But who am I kidding. This is not the ballet we are

attending; this will be a party full of lights and people who will have advice and opinions and questions.

Every day this week, Pop has reminded me about Dr. Michael Frame. He is a PhD. He is a tenured professor. He is well regarded, published, consulted. He owns a house in Sheepshead Bay. A single house, just for his family. He comes, long ago, from my father's world. Now he lives in another. My father wants to join him. He desperately wants to join him.

"Ready?" he asks from my doorway.

Pop is holding my coat. It has lost all its magic, my purple suede *dublonka*, forced to accommodate a discounted dress that should really be worn in the summer.

Outside, the main drag of Brighton Beach is alive. Music and laughter spill from the restaurants, and ladies bearing plastic torches of carnations gabble and grip their companions, negotiating the snow on their stiletto boots. *Sasha, sweetheart, slow down, I beg you. If I wind up in the snow bank, you'll have to call the tow truck—that's how much I ate, I warn you!*

Pop hails a car, a "gypsy cab," they call them—the men in the long black sedans who are either en route to the airport or double-parked on the avenue eating meat pies.

"*Snovim Godom,*" the driver greets us. "Happy New Year! Slam that door hard—HUP—like your old lady's ass, and off-we-go-here-we-go-let's-go-where-to?"

Pop brushes snow from his bare head and gives the driver an address that means nothing to me and my ten-block zone of familiarity.

"Okay," says the chauffeur, slamming the gear stick

down. He holds his peace for exactly one traffic light before he bursts out: "Excellent holiday, New Year's. Just a one-hundred percent excellent holiday. Oh, don't worry; I won't be working all night. No, you won't find me making hay while the sun shines. I haul ass year round so I don't have to be the mule on New Year's. Nope. You folks will be my last fare. So don't be shy to tip heavy. It all goes to the wife and kids tonight. Champagne, fireworks, and couple more bullshit *vietnamski* plastic buggers for the tree. New Year's! My stash is already put away, you know."

Pop murmurs that that's all good. Just fine. New Year's.

"Been driving for more than six years now, myself. And what's your line of business, if I may ask?"

I'm surprised at how promptly Pop answers. I had thought that the answer was uncertain to all of us, my father included. But he says without hesitation, "Pharmaceuticals."

Pharmaceuticals? I think. *So is that who we are tonight?*

Pop is looking out the window, one arm across the back of the seat and the other hand gripping the strange handle above the door, peculiar to American cars. Do they drive so fast that passengers need to both sit and hang on?

As if to answer, our garrulous driver takes a wide turn at high speed, and I tumble into Pop's lap.

"That right?" asks the front seat. "Let me guess—Johnson and Johnson?" It comes out Djonsoon and Djonsoon, so I don't immediately think of the big yellow bottle and the baby with a head full of suds that they advertise during the soap operas.

But Pop has changed his story. Maybe because of my quizzical look.

"Well, I'm looking for work," he says, brushing my hair from his mouth. "We've just been here a month."

"*Blin*," hollers the front seat in surprise. "You don't look like newbies a bit. Believe me, I can spot the Sovogs in the blink of an eye, but you . . . and already hobnobbing in the Bay! Well done, I say."

Pop smiles, pleased.

We've come out into a broad avenue bordered on one side by small restaurants squatting under a highway and on the other by the scaffolded lighting of yachts at anchor. The effect is immediate; we've arrived somewhere new. It's lovely, this little Côte-D'Azur, right at the end of our Russian ghetto, and I suddenly have flashbacks of the port outside Athens and the moneyed lights of the ships that weren't meant for fugitives.

"Look, Marina," says Pop, but I already am, drinking up the twinkling glamour of the boats rocking in the black water.

"Yes—the marina. Pretty isn't she?" says our driver.

I feel very well disposed to this fellow now, like I should introduce myself—*yes, I'm also Marina, and my Pop is Viktor. And we are Joe Blows going to a party on the Bay.*

At the end of the marina, we take a right onto a tree-lined street. The houses here are lit up just as festively. All is quiet, the sound of revelry trapped behind closed doors.

"*Vot i priekhali* . . . this is it." The driver slams the gear stick into park and turns around. His round face is more intelligent than I had imagined from the back seat. He proffers his hand. "Yura Mashkov." he says.

Pop clasps it. "Viktor Ivanov."

Then Yura pulls a card from behind the sun visor and hands it to Pop.

"I don't mean nothing presumptuous Viktor, but chauffeurs do real well down here. Course, you have great things in store, I'm sure. But things have a way of going slow. Or going sour. Or just going. So don't be ashamed to give me a call. Always a pleasure to have an educated bloke at the wheel. People tip good when you've got some intelligent conversation, you know what I'm saying? Or just, you know, as another alternative, a pleasant disposition. Now you and your pretty daughter have a nice evening. May the New Year be prosperous, the vodka plentiful, and the *shvitz* enervating."

Pop gives Yura six dollars—a very big tip. I put it down to Yura's friendliness and not his use of the word "enervating." But when I climb out I see that Pop's jaw is clenched. His fist is, too, around the crumpled business card for Brighton Ideal Taxi and Limousine Service.

The front door opens before we reach the top of the steps, and a small storm of teenagers breaks over us. We squeeze against the railing as they take the stairs, shouting goodbyes and Happy New Years. I smell something spicy and exotic as one of them, a girl with short hair and large gold earrings, backs into me, her eyes still on the yellow square of the doorway.

"Oh, sorry," she gasps, turning and grabbing my forearms, as if to keep me from falling. "I'm so sorry."

"It's okay," I answer this unaccented apology.

She smiles, an open-mouthed American smile, and lets go of my arms. Her friends are doing cartwheels in the small yard. They shake their red hands and lick snow from their palms. More kids join the party, expelled from the doorway. The front steps are a ski ramp, the yard a disco of snowballs.

"Where's Ben?" asks the girl with the hoops in her ears.

"He'll be out in a second," answers a boy with long hair as he slaloms past. I take it all in, this collision with exuberance. It seems one party's ended and another begun.

My father shifts the bottle he has brought from one hand to another and climbs to the top of the steps. I stay put, watching two more figures fill the doorway. The taller one—a boy my age—wears a British style sailor's coat and a long red scarf. He leans slightly to kiss the other's cheek. "*Snovim Godom*, Pop," he says. "See you tomorrow."

Now he has stepped over the threshold, has his hand on the banister. He is next to me on the stairs, his bright eyes curious. I can tell they are a rich brown, like chocolate. He nods to me, hesitates for a moment, and smiles a crooked smile. His hair is a mop of curls, and I feel sure that the girl with the gold earrings is in love with him.

My father's voice slides into the doorway above us, and the host's voice catches it: "How wonderful you have arrived! Come in, come in!"

The boy in the sailor coat has slipped past me. He's on the bottom stair, scooping snow into his hand for a departing missile but suddenly, from the porch: "Ben, come back and meet our guests, just arrived from Moscow."

The boy turns and looks up at his father, who is ushering my father into the house. "Come on then, take the young lady's coat, and bring her in."

The yard is a tableau of surprised innocence. Changed plans. Trampled snow like unmade beds. There is no disappointment or defiance, just recalibration.

I see the girl take a giant step to stand closer to Benjamin Frame, who is looking, again, at me. I am frozen at the spot of my humiliation. Not just because I am poorly timed, newly arrived, and at a loss for words. Not simply because I am an obstacle, a barnacle on the railing, a slightly foreign creature that this boy should have expected, after all. But also because I feel certain that the other kids in the yard hang up their own coats when they come to the Frames' house. And that when they do, they are dressed in jeans and turtlenecks, not off-the-shoulder party dresses.

I grapple with mortification and pronounce, "Not necessary. No need for help me." It is the English of a Soviet tour guide. I hear a single snicker, a show of mirth that is funnier for not being restrained. I clamber up the steps, wanting to flee.

But Benjamin Frame says, in beautiful Russian, "Necessity is overrated. Hospitality is not." Then he says, in English even I can understand, "I'll see you guys later."

And if that is not surprising enough, the boy touches my shoulder when he helps me out of my coat. "I didn't catch your name," he apologizes.

"My name is Marina," I say.

IN RUSSIA WE GREET the New Year at a long laden table. We greet it rocking dangerously on a dozen kitchen chairs. We greet it with smoked fish and many bottles and six plates of meat and chopped liver and salads that are viscous, not leafy, and stick to the floor when you spill. We greet it with guitars and with songs. If we are all talking at once, we are still all part of a single party.

In Sheepshead Bay, Dr. Frame and his guests greet the New Year in small groups—some standing, some seated, some in Russian, and some in English. It's many parties within a party. There is a table of food (some Russian, some unrecognizable), but no chairs to pull up to it and tuck in. I watch, fascinated, as a fat man in a plaid jacket takes a plate from one end of the table and fills it, slowly and thoughtfully, from the various platters. Then he picks up a plastic fork and wanders over to a small group of people gazing out the glass door at the back end of the marina.

There is a low, civilized hum of voices, an occasional burst of laughter, and some jazzy music playing that could be very modern or very Western. It could also just be the musical version of the wallpaper that frames the blazing fireplace and the room's heavy bookshelves.

"What can I get you to drink?" asks Benjamin Frame. "Champagne?"

I nod, grateful.

He fetches a glass and watches me sip. I wish he had one as well, but he just stuffs his hands in his pockets. "How about something to eat?"

The idea is ludicrous. "Not just yet," I say.

"Well, when you're ready, I recommend the chicken skewers. And the caviar is for real, too. But the quiche . . ." he screws his face into a grimace and gestures with his hand like it's a boat that's about to capsize. I smile. I have no idea what "quiche" is.

"Where were you going?" I ask. "I mean, where will you meet your friends?"

"Oh, who knows. They were going to someone's house and then, who knows. We sort of like a New Year's crawl, you know? We bounce from place to place."

I nod.

"So . . . just got here, huh?" he asks.

"About a month," I say. I don't offer any more details. The ones that are true are secret. The ones that are false don't even bear telling.

"It's better here," he says. "You'll see."

I nod again. I can't get my bearings, standing in the middle of the room. Ben takes my glass. I can't believe it's empty.

"You need to catch up," he says, smiling.

I watch him pull a bottle from a large ice bucket near the table of food and fill the glass. As he does, his father approaches. They speak briefly. Ben glances at his watch. I try to turn my head before Dr. Frame looks at me, pretend I don't see them negotiating. I scan the room for my father, who is standing with another small group, listening intently. Now Dr. Frame approaches.

"Marina," he says, "Welcome to America. Welcome to our home. Let me introduce you to my wife. She will be glad to see a nice Russian girl in the house. She thinks our son has forgotten all his declensions, not to mention all his Pushkin."

Dr. Frame takes my elbow and steers me into another room, slightly smaller, where more people are watching the television set. They are sitting. They are standing. They are speaking in Russian—about Andropov and Reagan and the Iron Lady, Margaret Thatcher. I glance at the TV, but there's nothing there to suggest international politics. Just Times Square and the crowds of people who have congregated—none of them, I know, summoned by officials to do so.

Now we are in the hallway again, and there are more people arriving as others are leaving. Dr. Frame still has my elbow as he greets a middle-aged couple in English and, in Russian, rebukes those hunting for their coats: "I see how it is then, Andrei, I can see that you love your mother-in-law more than you love me. We'll just make a note: 'Andrei, absenteeism, failure to complete.'" The Andrei in question laughs, makes an off-color joke about Dr. Frame's own "failures to complete," bringing hoots and slaps from the woman leaving with him, who then smothers Dr. Frame with kisses and stumbles out the door. "Goodbye, Marina!" she shouts and I wonder how I missed being introduced in the middle of the joke.

Mrs. Frame is in the kitchen, a petite brunette

clattering about in her high heels and an apron, expertly decanting and adjusting and filling plates and serving dishes. She brushes a lock of dark hair from her flushed cheeks and glances up at me with interest. Her son, I see, got her looks. She continues to assemble food as she unleashes a river of questions running wild over rapids of opinions:

"Marina, *dorogaya*, what a beauty you are. Welcome. How do you like Brooklyn? From Moscow? Of course. Though you could pass for a Petersburg girl, with your poise. My father was from Petersburg, you see. He was an art historian, specialized in the Flemish masters. We had a flat overlooking the Hermitage. You were in the *vysotka*? Frightening building that, though a friend once brought me an astonishing fur from the furrier there— what's it called? You can't find silver fox like that here. But listen, what school will you be attending? Don't let them stick you in this Brighton ghetto school. They're good pedagogues of course, but astonishingly insular and not overly cultured. Not that Brooklyn Bay is much better, but at least you will not be in a little Russian bubble there . . .

"Many of Benjamin's friends from the neighborhood went to Brooklyn Bay. The ones without the sort of artistic training that Ben was fortunate to have. Don't worry about the language, *dorogaya*, ours always excel, Russians absorb it, pick it up. All new things. Before you know it, you will be two Marinas. It's true. Old Marina and new Marina and they will both be beauties, my dear . . . Lara, get the turnover out of the oven, will you?

"Our Ben was a child when we came, but he was fluent in a year. He's at Juilliard now, continuing his music. Do you play an instrument, dear? You look like a cellist. Doesn't she look like a cellist, Michael? Ben plays piano. He went to a music school in Manhattan, but he knows the other Brooklyn schools as well. There are a few decent music schools in Brooklyn and an astonishing number of private tutors. They're all Russian émigrés of course. I wouldn't choose anyone else for a teacher. Though there's something to be said for the . . . I think the tart needs cream, Lara dear . . . and my husband, he has many connections in academia, Marina, so you should . . . No Lara, the silver tray . . . You met our son Ben, Marina?"

"Yes, we've met."

He's next to me again, this time with two glasses. And his father has disappeared. Dina Frame brushes another curl from her forehead and reaches for the glass.

"Let's have that, then, I'm parched," she says. She holds the glass high and says to me, "*Snovim Godom*, Marina. May your New Year be fruitful and may your new life be full of astonishing experiences, love, comfort, and . . . happiness." She takes a swallow and hands the glass back to her son, who nods both glass and curly hair at me and drinks also.

"Thank you," I say to this kitchen full of warm wishes. "*Snovim Godom* to you, too."

"Doesn't she look like a cellist?" Ben's mother asks. She pushes the kitchen door with her hip and departs, both hands full of turnovers.

Ben polishes off the champagne and produces,

magically, another bottle. He refills my glass, and by the time I have finished it, I can't remember why I shouldn't divulge that I am not a cellist.

"I'm a ballerina," I hear myself proclaim.

"Bolshoi preparatory?" he clarifies, clearly impressed. "Well then why wouldn't you apply to an arts school? You should be at LaGuardia or Manhattan Arts. Hell, you should apply to the School of American Ballet or to Juilliard."

I wince. I've outed myself after just three glasses of champagne.

"Well, it's complicated," I say. "I couldn't exactly arrange an audition in advance, and references . . . well." I'm stumbling, confused about where the impediments are. "Put it this way. My father needs to use this as a fresh start. He needs to, you know, put that life behind him. In short . . . I'm sure you understand."

I'm pretty sure he doesn't, but Benjamin must live in a world full of people with complicated pasts. He can just take all the crazy emigration stories he knows, slice them, splice them, measure me by them—and I won't have to say very much more.

"Your mother?" he asks. I shake my head.

He waits a beat. "My understanding is that your father works in my dad's field. Maybe . . ."

"Do you feel like an American?" I blurt, hoping to change the subject.

He takes a breath. Puffs his cheeks at this sudden detour.

"Well, I was nearly ten when I came. My friends are all American."

I don't know if it's a confession or a warning.

"But they make me feel Russian. Sometimes," he says.

"There is nothing here for me," I say after a pause. "At least, nothing that I know of. We had a plan once, but my mother . . . well, it changes things, you know. So I don't know what my plan is anymore. And my father is . . . he can't just . . . He can't do what he did. Before."

The cook or helper or whatever she is, Lara, has come back through the kitchen door. It swings back and forth like in a Western saloon. Through it I catch a glimpse of Pop standing alone in front of the television. I'm drunk. I've said too much.

"You should probably go meet your friends now," I say. "They must be wondering . . ."

Ben is quiet. He's running his finger around the top of the glass, pulling a low, but audible ring from the crystal. I copy him. But my glass is still half full, so the pitch of the hum is higher. We do this, harmonizing glasses.

"You're in a bad way," he says in English, not looking up, not breaking the sound.

You don't know the half of it, I would say, but I don't know the expression yet.

IT'S NEARLY MIDNIGHT AND I'm in Ben's bedroom. This is also very un-Russian. Bedrooms are not for parties. Unless of course, your flat is so small that you sleep on the couch. That changes the equation. But it's not like you can call that a bedroom. Certainly not a strange boy's bedroom where you can close the door and be alone.

It's clear that Ben doesn't think there's anything

strange about us being in his room when the party is downstairs. He seems perfectly comfortable. Almost. I guess I mean that he would be perfectly comfortable, if only I were, too.

We're here, ostensibly, to listen to music. It started when I explained that not only am I not a cellist, but I'm not a musician at all. Some ballerinas take music theory or play the piano a bit. I like the piano, as long as it isn't Tchaikovsky or Chopin or Shchedrin. He laughed and said there's a lot more piano that is *not* Tchaikovsky or Chopin or Shchedrin than *is* Tchaikovsky or Chopin or Shchedrin, and I said, "Well then, you see, I like the piano. Almost all of it." Then he started asking me if I liked this guy or that guy, and I had trouble knowing if he was asking if I liked this guy's music, or this guy's playing, and it was clear that we had very different source lists to draw from for this subject, and it was beginning to get pointless. I glanced across the room and saw my father talking to Dr. Frame. Something in their body language told me their conversation was hitting the same obstacles. I saw Dr. Frame glance at his watch.

"Stevie Wonder," said Ben.

"What?" I asked, "Sorry. Who?"

"Little Stevie Wonder," he said. "Started recording at age thirteen. Greatest living keyboard player today. And songwriter. He's blind. R&B, you know. Soul?"

"Soul," I said, thinking. "No."

So that's why I am sitting on Benjamin Frame's bed.

"*Songs in the Key of Life*—his fifth album. Released

in nineteen seventy-six," he says. I take in the clues
that litter this room. A window with a broken blind. A
standing lamp with an arched neck, its bulb illuminating
just the bed and a bedside table, piled with books. I see
English titles: History of this and that, but also a novel
by Bulgakov. Ben's bed is made, though the pillows look
as though he has just rolled off them. Against the window is his electric keyboard. Sheet music is strewn on
the floor beneath, and I can see some handwritten music
on the bench. Ben fancies himself a composer. I scan
the walls: a few posters of bands and musicians, none I
recognize.

"Songs in the key of life," I repeat, "That must be
some crazy cacophony."

Ben glances at me from where he is crouching—in
front of the most complicated stereo set I've ever seen.
There is a turntable, a cassette deck and a reel-to-reel
tape machine. Three different control panels sit atop the
deck; the top one glows green like a submarine dash-
board. Next to the turntable, I see a mixing board,
stripped of all the numbers and writing. Just a black
box of levers, the hi-fi abacus of a man of great musical
confidence.

"Nope. This is a blind man who only sees light. He
can't play a wrong chord." He drops the needle on Stevie Wonder.

"Really? There are so many wrong chords in
the key of life." I say. But Ben sits next to me and
shushes me, one finger on his lips. He leans back
on his hands and gazes at the ceiling. Pretty soon

he's singing along, and I feel like they've both forgotten I'm there—Stevie and Ben. I try to make out the words. I hear "mystery" and "joy" and "pain," and then I stop listening.

My eyes wander to the desk, hidden outside of the big lamp's penumbra. There's a photograph in the corner, framed. It's of Ben and someone that I think might be the girl with gold earrings.

"*Al-ways . . . Al-ways . . . Al-ways.*"

Ben has stood up. His head is shaking and his hands are moving like they are trying to catch something. The song has shifted, and I'm beginning to understand. Stevie Wonder is serenading, I think, himself. I can hear his confidence and his certainty, so I try harder to understand what he's saying, but all I know for sure is that this is no lazy melody with sweet lyrics. This is a whispering, panting, many-voiced creature winding a spring somewhere deep in the chorus. Somewhere deep in my gut. I'm caught in a whirlpool of anticipation. I imagine an ancient ritual, a church full of incense, a trance of certainty, love, abandon. I close my eyes, swaying, and breathe it in. By now Stevie Wonder is yelling in the key of life, and I'm ready to spin all the way down the causeway of the marina on Sheepshead Bay, because Stevie Wonder just can't stop telling me that he'll be loving me always. Always. Always.

And then the song is over. Ben is looking at me, waiting for my reaction.

"Mutual," I say in English. "The feeling is mutual. I will love Stevie Wonder always."

Ben's smile is Russian, which means it is restrained, but I can feel that it restrains something huge. I can tell that now he really is perfectly comfortable.

From downstairs we hear the countdown: *Ten—nine—eight . . .*

"Shall we?" he asks, cocking an eyebrow.

I shrug. We don't move. The needle bumps and bumps against the end of the song. Only when the shouting of *Happy New Year!* ends and the singing begins do we decide that we should join the party downstairs.

It's 12:06, January 1, 1983.

SEVEN
PIANO MAN

"I'm not sure why. That's just how it is. The Kinks, The Cars, The Cure, but just plain Rush. Journey, too—no *the*. And you can say The Stones leaving out 'Rolling' but not The Heads. It's The Talking Heads . . . or sometimes, without *the*—just 'Talking Heads.'"

I follow Ben through the aisles of records, each in a chest-level bin, organized by genre and, within those, alphabetically: The Ramones are under R; The Smiths, S; The Who, W. Asia, Blue Oyster Cult, and Foreigner . . . no *the*. It's confusing for a Russian. We don't use articles at all. In Russian, any foreigner is *a foreigner* and *the foreigner* and collectively *foreign* all at the same time. But in America, even foreigners can be individuals. And can make albums that are on the Top Ten charts.

Ben pulls me away from Foreigner as quickly as he had re-routed me from the comfort of The Beatles. I know all of The Beatles. We passed them around with abandon at

home. Even kids who knew zero English could plead
Love, Love me do. The Beatles were a revelation for us,
giving us a glimpse into truths much more international
than Marxism and the primacy of the proletariat. But
Ben calls them "overrated." I disagree hotly, but find I
don't have the words to defend them, since there's never
been any reason to do so before. In the end, Ben buys an
album called *Piano Man.*

Outside he presents it to me. "For your edification,"
he says. "True, the title track is a little maudlin, but this
man is truly a keyboard genius. Just skip the first song."

It's a week since we first met, and I don't know why,
but Benjamin Frame has taken me under his wing. Under
his wing, into Manhattan and all the way to Lincoln
Center. (The *real* Lincoln Center.)

We've just come from the apartment of Milton Krespky, a professor at Juilliard, the arts school where Ben
will return after vacation. "He's a composer—mostly
schlock show tunes," Ben had told me in advance. "But
he's in good with the dance department. And Juilliard's
dance department is practically in bed with ABT, so it's
definitely worth a shot."

He'd called in advance. When we arrived at the seventh floor of a proud old building not far from Lincoln
Center, a small balding man in fussy clothes opened the
door.

"Hello Benjamin, just couldn't stay away?" asked
Krespky, his voice dripping with boredom. Then he
peered at me over narrow glasses and ushered us into a
room full of librettos and cats.

Ten minutes later I had an appointment at Juilliard.

"Monday at four thirty with Greta von Schlief in studio four," Krespky said, after he made the smacking sound of an air-kiss into the phone and hung up. "Marina, I do hope you will make me look like a genius for discovering another prodigy." Then he rolled his eyes at Ben, "Benjamin, my pigeon, don't be a stranger. Give my love to your mother. Now if you will excuse me, I have a date with *Evita*."

We pulled on our coats and left. As we waited for the elevator we heard Krespky singing "Don't Cry for Me Argentina," with all the pathos of a doomed diva.

"Like I said," Ben mumbled, as if in apology. "He's in good with the dance department."

We celebrated with pizza in Greenwich Village, and now I'm getting a lesson in popular American music. I tell Ben that I thought Americans all listen to rock and roll.

"Ye-e-es," he acknowledges, in the voice of a physicist who is about to tell you to abandon all of the fundamentals that you've previously been taught. Then he explains to me about alternative music and the balance between "pop" and "popular." He clarifies that punk music, even though it is anti-pop, is still very popular. This puts it outside of "alternative" even while it is "anti-establishment."

"Trust me, Sid Vicious and Iggy Pop are doing just fine in record sales," says Ben. We trudge through the sludgy grey streets. "Some music is cynical, but not subversive. It makes a big show of not wanting to be liked.

It wants to scare people away. But I don't really believe that crap. Every musician wants to be acclaimed in some way. And plenty of music that tries to break the mold turns out to be the new thing, right? Funk is like that. Rap music, too. It's black music, but so was ragtime and blues and soul, right?"

Ben's forearm shoots out and prevents me from stepping into a tsunami sent up by a passing delivery truck careening through a gutter puddle. Bad drivers are something Moscow and New York have in common.

"Take Stevie Wonder and Billy Joel," he continues, not missing a beat. "Both at the pinnacle of popularity, and why? Because people want to sing their songs in bars and in the shower, and because their piano skills are superlative. Like the black blues players and rag pianists before them. Good lyrics. Great keys."

"Who's Billy Joel?" I ask.

Ben pulls him from the shopping bag, and I take a closer look at the piano man, resting on his elbow and gazing at me with hound-dog eyes. He bears a resemblance to some of our *Estrada* heartthrobs. Yes, he has a dark complexion and thick lips, but I would have thought he was just Jewish.

"He's black?" I ask.

Ben laughs. "Uh, no. And that's important, see. Stevie Wonder can be popular without being pop. Billy Joel will have to work hard not to let his popularity get lazy. Then he becomes pop, too. See?"

"Sure." I say. But I just think, *pop: lazy*.

It's getting dark, and Ben is going to meet Lindsay, the

girl with the gold earrings. He asks if I want to come, too. I'm pretty sure it doesn't matter to him whether I say yes or no, but I haven't figured out whether that says more about Lindsay or about me.

LINDSAY HAD BEEN WITH Ben on New Year's Day when I ran into him on the boardwalk. He hadn't even tried to act like it was an accident, his being in my neighborhood less than twenty-four hours after I'd had left his.

"This is Lindsay." He introduced us in English. "She's at Brooklyn Bay High, which is where you will be going if you don't do anything about it before next week. I brought her to help talk you out of it."

"You *sooo* don't want to go to Bay," she said. "It is totally lame." And then she told me about the gangs and the drugs and the teachers who disappeared for days at a time and didn't have substitutes. She told me about the police at the entrance and about how the only arts classes were "jazzercise" and "macramé."

"Macramé?" I asked. "That is pasta dish?"

"Oh, and don't even get me started on the home-ec front. They will, Marina, make you take home ec as an incoming new student."

"So why don't you go somewhere better?" I asked.

"Oh, it's totally not like that for me," Lindsay said. "It's just part of my story, right? Makes me legit. I'm not a fancy pants composer, and I'm not Euro-intelligentsia. I'm all Brooklyn, baby." She smacked her gum and winked at me, though I could tell she was really looking at Ben.

"That's why she wears so much patchouli," he dead-panned.

Then he had suggested that we go get tea.

At the café, Lindsay was just as flirtatious with me as she was with Ben—who kept the conversation flowing, translating where necessary, giving examples and analogies where helpful. We'd gone through two pots of tea and a massive piece of dried-out coffee cake ("It's not bad if you dunk it in the tea," Lindsay insisted) when the door flew open. A man with a face like a chainsaw walked in flanked by two enormous specimens of a type I recognized immediately. At that point, Ben stopped speaking Russian entirely. Lindsay leaned in and said "*bratva?*" with a question mark. Ben hushed her.

"Something else for you to know about your new neighborhood," he whispered to me in English.

I tracked the men's confident course across the café to a corner table; watched the peroxide blonde waitress spit her gum out and straighten her hair before approaching; heard the guy in the middle order 500 grams in a carafe and a plate of pickles, with a curt: "And tell Vova I've arrived."

These were unmistakable *vori v zakone*. What we call "thieves of the law"—the law, of course, being strictly of the thieves' fashioning, not the court's. But in Brighton, I learned that day, they are called mafia. Specifically, because they are Russian mafia, they are called *bratva*, the brotherhood.

"I just love the *bratva*," Lindsay confessed, once we'd paid for our tea and headed back out into the cold. "I mean, *sooo* much tougher than the Italians. The second- and third-generation mob in Brooklyn today? The Godfather would be ashamed to listen to some of them, you know? Like, 'Oh there goes my retarded grandson—he's such a disappointment,' you know what I mean? I can say that because I'm Italian. Plus the Russians? None of them are cokeheads and they can all hold their liquor."

"You don't know what the fuck you're talking about, Lindsay," Ben muttered, huddling into his jacket.

Lindsay just rolled her eyes at me and smiled, but that was the end of that conversation.

"HER BAND IS PLAYING a set nearby," Ben is telling me now as we stand on the corner near the subway. "You can come, but I don't know if you're going to like the music that much. Lindsay likes to think she's Joan Jett, but . . . well, there's more attitude than acumen there, you know? But if you're really into rock and roll, maybe you should. We could call your dad." He pauses. "Unless you still don't know your number."

He's teasing me. He had asked for my number on New Year's Eve, and I had no idea what it was. He had shrugged and told me: "No biggie. Look me up if you want." But he said it in English, and I didn't know what it meant.

"It's seven-one-eight-four-four-four-three-one-two-one," I say now. "Remember it."

Then I soldier on, using English to thank Benjamin Frame for, well, for everything. "I'm going home to rest and to practice my father for audition. I am grateful for your . . . invocation? I mean, introduction?" Ben nods and rolls his hands in the universal symbol to continue. "I will do best to make you like genius ballet scout."

Ben laughs. "Good luck on Monday," he says.

I feel my heart sink, suddenly wondering if maybe that's it. That, having secured this opportunity at Juilliard, Ben is finished with me. When what I want is for him to come with me, stay with me, hold my hand all the way to Lincoln Center like Sveta would have.

"Wait," I say.

He waits.

I hesitate. "I don't have record player," I say finally, holding the shopping bag high as a reference.

He drops his head and his curls are laughing at me. "I have boom box only," I add, like it's an apology.

"Then I will make you a tape," he says.

Benjamin Frame takes the album from my hand, kisses me quickly on the cheek, and walks away, a piano man headed deeper into the Village and its cynical music.

THAT AFTERNOON, ALL THE way home to Brooklyn, I am thinking only of Monday: the day I find out what macramé is, whether Lindsay will still be my friend in the "legit" halls of Bay High, and whether I can run away from it all on my toe shoes. Ben and his snooty composer have given me a chance. Now as I feverishly remember that I need tights, a leotard, a selection of choreographies to run through, I wonder if I will be ready. A ballerina's muscles can atrophy in a month with disuse. Not to mention her spirit.

The train is crossing the river into Brooklyn. I gaze out on the constellation of my new city at night as it spills out on either side of the river. A solitary tugboat, like the first summer firefly, blinks its way on the dark winter water. We slide into the first station above ground. The doors open to take bundled-up Brooklyn home, and the frigid air comes in, too. As we push further into the borough, the temperature drops and the buildings, just like molecules reacting to cold, move farther apart. Before long I can smell the half-frozen salt of the ocean. I'm running the allegro from *Don Quixote* through my head, my hands marking the leg movements, my feet tapping beats.

I'm the last one off when we reach Brighton Beach. I dawdle, allowing the passengers to exit, and then I have the platform alone to rehearse Dulcinea's final leaps down the platform. All the way down five blocks of Brighton Beach Avenue, I am a fiery Spaniard, melting the crusts of ice in the gutter. I mount the stairs, snapping at each door flamenco-style.

Pop is at home, making more macaroni. I spill all my news before I've even hung up my coat. He wipes his hands, pulls a cigarette from the pack with his teeth. He has a million questions. Where is this Juilliard? What will it cost? Do they give scholarships? What have I said about my ballet training in Moscow? What have I said about Svetlana?

I'm rattled. I hadn't even thought about money. Or questions, or anything beyond what I will wear and what I will dance.

He shakes his head. "It's not safe, Marya. I don't know

about this Juilliard, but if it is part of American Ballet, that place is a defector's den. They're all there. Starting with Baryshnikov and Godonov and all the other nancies. The whole place is a pit of traitors. You better believe it's crawling with ours, too. Informants. Marya, you will bring danger on us if you raise your chin high in their midst."

I'm shocked. My father has just drawn a line that prevents me from standing on either side. Or maybe I'm not shocked. Maybe I'm angry.

"Have you completely forgotten why we left? Why we are here? If *they* are traitors, so are we. We abandoned our country, Pop. You and me both." My eyes are burning and it's all I can do not to add, *we abandoned my mother, too.*

But he's right. The state of the American Ballet is such that no one can dance there on the strength of art only. Not as long as the Cold War takes prisoners of culture. Dancers of that caliber, and especially ours, are pawns. All the more so once they trade sides and find themselves irrevocably on the front line. And those who would be Queen? Either they are toppled or they attack. There is no other role for a Queen.

"I will work hard," I whisper. "I will make it possible. I will be our anchor here, you'll see. Pop, please don't make me disappear."

He drops his cigarette in the sink and holds his head with both hands. I press my case. "There is Ma to think of. How are we going to get her back if we keep hiding? If we make a move, and we succeed . . ."

". . . they may send her here to lure us home?" he finishes.

It seems all the air has been sucked out of the kitchen.

I turn and hang up my coat in the closet by the door. Then I sit on the stool and pull off my boots, with their ragged shorelines of street-salt and snow. I'm working out my next argument, rethinking every motive I have to attend this audition, to expose myself for examination. My father steps from the kitchen and watches me, his hands deep in his hair.

"You're right," he says finally. "*Ti prava*, Marina. As long as there is a chance that we can save her, we use our resources. But understand, *dochka*, you are committing yourself to be a student of dance and also of intrigue." He kneels, holds both my hands in his. "You will hear things, you will be told things, and you will report back. You will keep your head low throughout: Marina Ivanov of the Bolshoi school, of Uzhgorod in Outer Mongolia."

I laugh, a short snort.

"I mean it, Marina," he says sternly, his grip on my hands tightening. "If you want to play this game, you will play it smart. I will not bring the KGB to my door until I can stand on my own and ask for something in return. You're right about that. Because they will be there. They will be there as surely as I am standing here. Do you think that they asked you dance for them because they need another set of Russian legs, Marya? Do you? So you play it down low. You stumble through your first semester and you play dumb while you get smart. You want to jump with the big boys and girls? You listen and learn. You find out what is happening before it happens, can you do that, Marya?"

Can I do that?

I could tell him. Tell him again. *Yes, Pop, sometimes I think that I can do just that.* But I am too amazed right now at the transformation that has come over him—my hapless father turned calculating and ruthless.

"Is this what you want, Pop?" I ask.

He doesn't answer. After a minute he drops my hands and turns his back. "Did Benjamin Frame say anything about me?"

"About you?" I ask, confused.

"Yes. Did he say anything about me? Has his father said anything?" he asks again. "Has Benjamin's father asked about me?"

"No," I answer. "But it's hardly even the end of the holiday, Pop. Ben's on vacation and he's got nothing better to do than to show me around. And his dad won't be able to do much for you till he gets back to work. Be patient."

"Maybe he lost my number," mutters my father, returning to the stove. "Make sure you mention it when you see him again, ok?"

"*Da*, Pop," I say. And at this moment, I mean it. I am, apparently, not only a traitor and a spy, but an operative of my own future. I'm a mess of motives.

MONDAY ARRIVES. POP INSISTS on walking me the five blocks north to Brooklyn Bay High. He observes the red brick building with the bars across the windows, the elaborate entryway that wants to be a portal to a medieval gated city, and says, "Cheerful sort of place."

I kiss him on the cheek and remind him to pay the gas bill.

"See you tonight," he says.

I'm halfway across the street before I shout back, "I'll be late." I don't want to remind him about the audition. About Juilliard. About my ambivalent entry into the dancing snake pit up at Lincoln Center.

Inside the entry of Bay High I paddle my way through a sea of backpack-dragging teenagers unenthusiastically beginning a new semester. I find the office, where I am eventually greeted by someone who calls herself assistant principal and hands me a sheet of paper with classroom numbers and a schedule. I arrive at class 404 fifteen minutes into the start of the day.

"Marina Ivanov," announces the teacher, and though she isn't Russian, it is clear that she is familiar with us and our names and the reticence of our newly-arrivedness. She points to a desk on the far side of the room and tells me to take a seat.

Over the next three hours, I learn these things: In America, high school seniors read novels to study government, make pastry in a semblance of learning French, solve mathematical problems using calculators, but do the bulk of their information-gathering at their lockers between classes.

This is where Lindsay finds me during the break between third and fourth period.

I am battling the combination lock when she sidles up alongside me, smelling again of that strange cloying spice that I had first noticed on New Year's Eve.

"Hey! I heard you were here today. Matt Kowalski noticed you. Said there was a "brown-haired Red" in his French class, isn't he the cleverest? So how's it going? What do you think? Is it as awful as I promised?"

I want to tell her that when you are hurtling down river on a paper boat, you don't really notice the passing shoreline. This—the dank halls and low roar that is Bay High—is just the periphery. The audition that follows is the precipice. My worries begin at 3 P.M., when the countdown begins. With only ninety minutes to get from here to home to the subway to Manhattan to studio four, that's when I will know "how it is going."

Instead I say, "Good."

Lindsay watches me fumbling with the combination on my locker. "Let me help. Spin right, pass left, direct right, okay? So it's, what? Eighteen . . . then you go all the way past twenty to twenty again and then, zoop, to ten and *voilà*." The locker springs open and a pair of dingy white boy briefs falls out.

"Now, that's just grody," Lindsay says with a laugh. "Listen, I'll meet you in the cafeteria at lunch, okay?" She dispatches the former locker owner's underwear down the dark hallway with an expert kick and then disappears in the other direction.

I find my way to a science lab, reminiscent of a lab only in that we sit at high counters on stools and have to navigate a deep (but dry) sink to take notes. In the next class, the civics teacher asks me if I would like to describe for the class the electoral system in the Soviet Union. There are snickers all around, and I think, *Tattoo You, civics guy.* Instead, I say, "The electoral system in the Soviet Union is . . . uncontested." The civics teacher nods, a slight smile on his face. "Good answer. Class, this is our newest student, Marina Ivanov."

At lunch Lindsay introduces me to a bunch of her friends, and I don't catch any of their names except for one: Masha. She speaks very strange Russian and quizzes me about which building I live in on Brighton Beach Avenue.

"That one's mostly old folks," she explains. "Brighton Four is for politicals and dissidents. Brighton Five is like, totally Jewish and so is Brighton Two. And anything between the Baths and the Bay is mafia."

Lindsay leans in. "Oooh—are you talking about the mafia? Masha has uncles in the *bratva*, don't you, Masha? They have all these racehorses over in Mill Basin, and they sell them for like, a gazillion dollars and they smuggle booze and have some oil thing going. Oh my god, we went out to a nightclub once with them . . . Whose wedding was it, Masha? And these guys wanted one of the private rooms that was already taken and they just kicked the table over and were like, 'Sorry friend, you've just soiled your—' What did they say Masha?"

But Masha just readjusts her headband and sniffs. "Lindsay is very imaginative," she says to me. It strikes me as only slightly more diplomatic than, "Lindsay doesn't know what the fuck she's talking about."

After lunch I begin to sweat. I've nearly completed the first day of school without a single misstep, but the triumph of this accomplishment is lost on me. It's 150 minutes until my audition, and the clock is ticking. All day long I've been doing the math: fifteen minutes to get home and grab my things. Fifty minutes to Manhattan. That's 4:10 P.M., *if* the train is waiting and *if* I don't bother to change my clothes at home. That leaves me twenty minutes to get from the train to the school, find Greta von Schlief, change into my dance clothes and take a deep breath. It's not enough time and there is nothing I can do but wait to be late.

I fidget through English, unable to concentrate on the discussion about Hemingway even though I've read all of his stories. (*I should change at home . . . I should go straight to the train . . . I should take the express . . . I should run for the local . . . I should call Yura the gypsy taxi guy . . . I should resign myself to fate.*) And now it's time for the long-promised home economics class, and fate hands me a free pass. Home ec is held in the "annex," a building that looks like the tool shed at our dacha, located outside in the schoolyard. I'm halfway there when I realize that macramé, as mysterious as it is, is not the priority right now. As discreetly as I know how (and I am Soviet, raised on discretion), I exit the schoolyard, cross the street, and bolt for the Avenue.

I race the five blocks home and drop my keys three times before getting the door open. I pound down the hallway. After I wash my face and put on lipstick, mascara, and eyeliner, I check the clock. Three P.M.: plenty of time. I double-check my dance bag—pale pink tights, a long sleeve black leotard, sheer short skirt. My shoes are spooned tightly together, bundled with their long ribbons. A box of lamb's wool, bobby pins, and hair elastics. Numerous adhesives, brilliant inventions they call Band-Aids. And there is a white rose made of silk as well, just in case.

In the kitchen I leave a note for Pop and drink a tall glass of water. I check the clock again: 3:08 P.M. I chug another glass to make myself pee. Mission accomplished. I grab my dance bag and my coat and lock the door behind me. I'm halfway down the stairs when I reconsider. In a flash I am back inside, a *grand jeté* down the hallway. I grab my Walkman from under my pillow. Now I am ready.

The train is waiting when I rush up the stairs to the platform. I take my favorite place in the head car and press play. It's a long ride to Lincoln Center but I'm already there: (*I'm Marina Ivanov. I will be performing Dulcinea's allegro from* Don Quixote.) All the way up the Coney Island line, I ride on my toes, marking my ground with a flick of wrist, dancing in the key of life.

I exit at Columbus Circle. There is an ache in my groin, half pleasurable and half painful. I either have to pee again or . . . something.

The sky is overcast and a crowd has gathered at the corner of the park where a horse and carriage has collided with a taxi. I weave my way through the rubberneckers and draw up short at a police barricade.

"Street's closed," shouts a cop, cap drawn low over his eyes. "Detour around Fifty-ninth and up Columbus."

I check my watch: 4:10 P.M. I'm off like a shot; the ache more like the feeling in the pit of your stomach when the roller coaster crests the top before the plunge. I hustle past slow-moving children, a human chain of puffy coats with a single eagle-eyed adult at their head, and fly around the corner with a backward glance. Benjamin taught me to check for uptown buses, but the street is empty. I won't run. Not yet. Again, that odd flush between my legs.

At 63rd the light is late yellow and I sprint across the avenue and up the wide steps toward the sleeping fountain at the heart of Lincoln Center. I'm halfway across the plaza when I see a familiar ensemble moving toward me: five girls, five long necks, five neat buns at their nape. Five bags slung across flat chests like bandoliers. Five dancers crossing the plaza with perfect turnout and supreme confidence. One hangs behind to fish a smoke from her bag. I make a beeline for her.

"I need to get to Juilliard, studio four."

She has liquid blue eyes. "See those stairs?" She is pointing across the street at a large complex of concrete and glass. "Up those, through the first door and all the way down the corridor. There will be a guard. Ask him."

When I arrive at the information desk and ask for Greta von Schlief, it is 4:25 P.M., and my crotch is wet.

And then I'm told to wait.

"Could I use a dressing room?" I ask.

The guard is on the phone. "Says it's for an audition?"

he says. Then he hangs up and points. "That way." More hallways, more dancers, and a mélange of piano keys. In the small dressing room, I quickly change, tucking my fingers discreetly into the fork of my tights. Tissues, soap. My hair is in a smooth knot at my neck. I pull out the flower and secure it behind my ear. Just as I do, three more dancers enter, chattering and stretching. They look me up and down. I ignore them and focus on lacing my shoes. I'm on my feet, banging toes to floor like a restless racehorse when one of the girls asks, "Are you here for auditions?"

"Yes," I say.

"Well, they usually begin with an interview. Did they tell you to prepare something?"

I can't fully process this. I've come to dance. Not to be interviewed. I've come to hold my chin high, while keeping my head low. I can't answer questions. I'm wearing a silk rose in my hair.

They are looking at me curiously, but not unkindly.

"I'm Marina Ivanov. I will be performing Dulcinea's *allegro* from *Don Quixote*," I say, managing to stop before I clap at the girl.

Her eyes widen, and she hides a smirk behind her fingers. Next to her, one of her friends says, "Okaaaay, then."

"Well, good luck," says the girl. "If you're here for von Schlief, you'll need it."

I beat a hasty retreat, my confidence in chaos. I'm halfway down the hall when the girl pokes her head back out and offers: "Red door, end of the hall."

I am about to thank her when the red door at the end of the hall opens to reveal a tall woman wearing a shapeless black dress accessorized by a chest full of long African-style beads. They look heavy enough to sink a corpse, but she stands ramrod straight, counterbalanced by a bouffant of iron grey hair. From among the whirlpool of beaded necklaces, she plucks a pair of spectacles attached to a braided cord and peers at me through the narrow lenses.

"Are you the one from Krespky?" she asks.

I nod.

"Well, clearly you mean to dance."

I'm standing before her now, unsure whether to drop a curtsy or just fall on one knee. "I'm sorry. I was told audition," I begin, already realizing with dismay that I was never told that. *4:30 P.M. with von Schlief*, he had said. *Studio four.* Von Schlief is still peering at me through her spectacles; I can see that the room behind her is in use. There is nowhere for me to dance. "Follow me," she orders, and I do.

We pass many practice rooms. The dancers wear ragged sweatshirts that hang from their shoulders like barbers' bibs. They wear leg warmers on one leg, leaving the other half clad, bare to the knee, tights full of holes. I see girls with toe shoes covered in graffiti; I see boys in athlete's shorts. I see an instructor place a young dancer's leg on his shoulder and trace a circle around her as she pivots smoothly on one heel, giving the entire class a full view of the rip in the crotch of her tights. I do not see a single short dance skirt, nor a single fake flower.

Von Schlief leads me into a wider hallway and up to a set of double doors. She holds one open, and I enter the cavernous dust-dark of an unused auditorium.

I wait, my heart pounding. Von Schlief walks past me down the left-hand aisle, past sleeping orchestra seats to the front of a full-size stage. She picks up a telephone on the wall and says, "This is von Schlief. I need an accompanist in the auditorium. That's right, main auditorium." Then she hangs up and climbs the short steps to the stage. She disappears stage left and leaves me with the familiar *thunk, thunk, chunk* of stage lights going on.

"Come on then," she calls from behind the curtain. "You can warm up. There's resin in the box."

I scramble down the aisle and jump onto the stage. Von Schlief pulls the curtains open, revealing a well-worn floor and a grand piano. I run through stretches, leaps, jumps, bang my shoes in the resin box. All the while von Schlief is firing questions. Have I had this training, that training, injuries, regimens, *pas de deux, pas de trois, pas de chat*, solos, tours? I answer yes to each one and then she pauses. "And is it true that you trained at the Bolshoi? Can you tell us anything about the present company? Anything about the delegation set to come later this month? Anything about Svetlana Dukovskaya's health situation?"

I freeze. Crack my neck. Trace a *rond de jambe* on the floor, stall. Pop is no dummy. Pop knows what they want.

"No," I say finally. "No, I can't."

Von Schlief drops her glasses back into the breastplate of beads. She frowns. From the back of the auditorium, the door slams.

"I understand you need an accompanist," echoes a familiar voice.

Von Schlief and I both turn and shield our eyes against the stage lights as Benjamin Frame, piano man, strides down the aisle. He jumps up on stage, runs his fingers over the keyboard, and looks at me expectantly.

I have never worked so hard to remain expressionless. Not even in the airport when Pop and I fled.

"I will be dancing Dulcinea's allegro," I say. Ben nods and begins to play.

And that's what I do. I dance.

EIGHT
JIVE TALKING

Three days after my full-court press on Juilliard, Brooklyn Bay High has a fire drill.

"A what?" I ask the girl who sits next to me in French class.

"A fire drill, girl. Dontcha have fires in Russia? Stop, drop, and roll yo ass outta da way?"

We're shivering in the schoolyard, coatless in the freezing air. A cold front has moved in. Lindsay crosses the yard to stand by me. "Hey, you," she says, as friendly as ever. "Ben says you might be ditching us. He says you blew them away at Juilliard."

I'm used to the way Lindsay talks now. How the things she says are her own version of the things that are said to her. So I don't know how to correct her without sounding like I'm correcting Ben, and in fact I don't know that either of them are wrong.

"Well, I sort of, what's the word? Sneak attack. I

mean they knew I was coming, but didn't know *I* was coming . . . you know what I mean?"

"Awesome," enthuses Lindsay. "That's totally punk rock. But listen. I mean, Juilliard is way awesome, for sure. But don't let it cramp your style. I always worry about Ben getting, you know, like, brainwashed by all that classical bullshit. I mean he's very avant-garde as a musician, and I'd hate to see him get, you know, all regimented and shit. His mom and I have a lot of disagreements about this." Her voice drops to a whisper. "He's starting to listen to *Billy Joel* for Christ's sake."

I nod, a stupid smile frozen on my face.

Lindsay rolls her eyes, just like a woman talking about her mother-in-law. I wonder, again, what she is to Ben. As if reading my thoughts she says, "But it will be great if you are there, too, Marina. You can keep an eye on him for me. Because I know he's got admirers . . . and not just that homo Krespky."

I nod, casually, like I never really doubted it, "So, you and Ben . . ."

"Oh yeah," she confirms. "He's my boy. We've been together forever."

A whistle blows and we file back into the building. Lindsay has risen in my esteem. Not because she is Ben's girlfriend, but because she knows how to mark her territory without baring her teeth. I respect that.

AFTER SCHOOL I RACE home and check the new answering machine that I insisted we install in case von Schlief should call in the middle of the day. But there's only the robot voice saying, "no new messages."

So I start on Pop's cake—his birthday cake. I'm measuring out flour and running through the conversation in von Schlief's office for the hundredth time: My performance indicated advanced training and natural strength of physical ability and plasticity. My tape, (yes, she had been taping the whole thing by remote camera) would be reviewed by her colleagues. She also had me fill out paperwork, very little of which I could complete, other than name, address, place of birth, and the information I'd memorized from Pop's fake passport. For mother, I simply wrote *deceased*. I told myself that I was a master deceiver and not a disloyal daughter. I told myself I wasn't a traitor. Ben was there: both interpreter and accompanist, and when von Schlief started talking about company fees and stipends, he interrupted. "Any information about financial aid and scholarship would be appreciated," he said. Von Schlief said she would be in touch before the end of the week.

Ben and I took the train home. Though he never used the phrase "blown away," his restrained Russian compliment said as much: *velikolepna*. Wondrous.

The phone rings and I jump. But it's just Pop. It's been a big week for him as well. He has a job. He has a car and a license, and he is earning dollars ferrying more fugitives the eleven miles from the airport to Brighton Beach. I'm proud of him. I'm actually pleased. Yes, it's a disappointment; it's also temporary. Sort of like Bay High and home ec and fire drills. I am certain that Pop will find a good job in a lab, maybe even a government lab. He just has to bide more time until we're sure that his secret is safe . . . that all of his secrets can be made safe.

"Marusya, can you hold dinner, *dochka*? I'm at JFK and I want to wait for the seven o'clock flight, get a good fare home."

"Sure, Pop. But not too late, okay? It's your birthday dinner."

I hang up and catch a fragment on the radio. News headlines. "Summit on arms control held in Geneva Switzerland . . . including international treaties to ban chemical and germ weapons . . . following recent revelations about secret test programs undertaken by Soviet researchers . . ." I scramble to the radio, wanting to hit rewind. But Americans don't linger on explanations. Already the man is talking about wildfires in Colorado and a recall of Tylenol.

I whip together the cake batter and put it in the oven. The chicken, I've decided, I will fry on the stovetop, along with potatoes and mushrooms. I'm peeling, paring, pondering.

In another hour the cake is out, cooling on the counter. The chicken is frying and I'm setting the table for two. My father's keys are in the lock and then I hear his voice: "Maruska, surprise! Look at my birthday present. Found it skulking around the baggage claim."

I raise my head. Dyadya Gosha is in the entryway.

"GEORGI, THE BASTARD, DIDN'T even have time to warn me. Just turns up at the airport on the seven o'clock. Another ten

minutes and he would have been hoofing it to a flop-
house on the bus, but, in short, I spied him, the bastard,
checking for quarters in the coin return on all the pay
phones. Doesn't even have a quarter, the bastard, to call
for a car!"

I'm watching Pop repeat his new favorite word
and swagger out of his coat, tossing pieces of his new
self on the table: keys, wallet, exaggerated hilarity
at the predicament of our Gosha, our newbie, whose
arrival has suddenly transformed my father into a
veteran American. And while part of me is sickened,
part of me is rooting for Pop. Because if he stops this
performance, he and I will both be at Gosha's knees,
crying out for reasons why he, too, has abandoned
our Sveta.

Now Gosha has hung up his coat and removed his
boots. He comes to me with a bouquet of flowers.

"For the lady of the house," he says and kisses me.
"Marya, it's good to see you. It's so good to see you."

He sits heavily at the table and shows me that he is
very tired. He is very sorry. He wants me to know it's
good that he's here.

I take the flowers into the kitchen, put them in a
vase. Then I turn down the burner under the chicken,
pull the bottle of vodka from the freezer, and pour
most of it down the kitchen sink. I want to hear at least
half of the truth tonight.

Soon we are eating, Pop and Gosha praising my cook-
ing more times than necessary. Pop fills glasses. There is
too much silence.

"Who will toast the birthday boy?" he asks, but Gosha raises a hand.

"*Nyet*, Vitya," he says quietly. "Let me speak about Sveta."

Pop drains his glass. Gosha and I do not.

"I saw her on New Year's Day. In a hospital not far from Lukino. The guards were easy to bribe—broke after the holiday; the nurses were mostly hungover. So I could see her. We had about twenty minutes."

I glance at Pop. His eyes are black with distrust. Green with envy. But mostly, they are full of tears. I wonder what he said to Gosha in his rented sedan as they drove home from the airport. Did he say, "*Please wait to tell me what's happened until there's a glass in my hand?*" Did he say, "*Don't worry, Gosh—you did your best, now leave it to me and Marya. We've got a scholarship and a gypsy cab license, what more do we need?*" Or did he just not ask. Afraid of the answer.

"She told me that she knew you were gone," Gosha explains. "She said she had 'seen' you leave. And she was very grateful. You have to know this . . . Sveta was very, very happy that you were gone. She told me this. She said 'Gosha, you have saved us. You have saved them and that is the only way to save me.' She said, 'Gosha, go with them.'"

Bullshit. I thought. It's my new favorite word.

"They had her medicated. But she was lucid because she told me to take down the details of everything she knew. About the incident at Lukino. And much more, Vitya. About the whole system. I have the notes with me. There are blanks. Not huge gaps, not holes, not guesses. Just gaps in a very straight story. She said only Vitya could fill them in. She said I needed to come and help you fill in these blanks and that with that information, with that knowledge, we would all be set free."

Pop pours more vodka. Or he tries. The bottle is empty.

"I don't know if I can," he says.

Through this enormous moment—this revelation that Gosha has dropped like a bomb on my homemade meal—neither one of them has glanced at me. But I am part of this story. I am part of this plan. And so I weigh in.

"What is this, Gosha?" I ask. "You're saying you left Ma alone to come and dig up more *kompromat*? That's your idea of making her safe? Some sort of cooked-up dossier from the Lukino research lab that will work like a magical incantation? Well shit, Gosh—why stop there?" I laugh, tapping depths of sarcasm. "Why not fly straight to Geneva and let them know there's a . . . what do they call them? The human rights hysterics? A prisoner of conscience! *Da*, a 'prisoner of conscience' that you abandoned, even though she's apparently only being guarded by drunks and bribe takers?"

My chest is heaving and I can feel an anguished sob, but I plough on, spitting chicken and hope and fear over the table. "Why not ring up the CIA and offer to sell them some germ weaponry in exchange for my mother? Or maybe we could bring a Hollywood producer back to Russia and he could offer the head of Lukino a major role in the movie version of *Whitewash at Lukino*, starring Svetlana Dukovskaya?"

"Hush, Marya," says my father. "We've discussed this. Moscow is looking for leaks. It's a miracle Georgi got out at all."

"Miracle? Where do you think the leak is, Pop?"

Pop rises and roots in his coat for cigarettes.

Gosha leans over and lays his hand on mine. It is not reassuring. He speaks words for me alone: "When there is no one to trust, Marya, you must make everyone believe that you trust only them. You watch, Sunshine. I will make it right. But you will not trust the steps I take. So take my advice. Make me believe that you trust me. Make me believe it, make your father believe it, and make every person that stands between you and your mother and your dreams believe it, too—that you trust only them. It's going to be a bumpy New Year, Sunshine. Let's come out of it ahead."

Then Gosha tells Pop that he's taking him out because he has to see for himself this famous "Brighton Beach," this "Little Odessa." And he has to buy Pop a birthday Budweiser. He pronounces the word with a leer—as if it is a court jester, or a lap dance: *Bood-viser!*

When they are gone I lift the birthday cake from the counter and pitch the whole thing into the trash. There is nothing, as far as I am concerned, to celebrate.

IT'S AFTER 10 P.M. An hour when radio surfing offers strange gifts. I'm looking for something to distract me. Something, maybe, to dance to. Instead I find monotonous

Jamaican music, blathering politicians, and an endless variety of women with sexy voices. I push the dial further to the end. Greek. Jazz flute. SABADO GIGANTE! I'm pretty sure it's not even Saturday. And then I find it: a small drumbeat that picks up a snare and tugs my hips. I stand at the window, grooving, and watch the train snake north, grooving too. "A snake," I think—in English. "Slippery snake, snake in the grass . . . slippery slope." Now the song on the radio has introduced a singer, and he has the voice of a snake. He whispers, falsetto, breathy and sneaky.

He has only one thing to say, and though I don't know what it is, I'm utterly seduced. I listen to the song to the end. Its chorus is repetitive enough that I can sing it by the time it's over. I want to know more, so without a second thought I call up Ben and sing it to him.

"Oh my God," Ben says when I'm done. "You need an intervention."

"Why?"

"Because you are smitten with the Bee Gees," he says.

"So? Not cool? Pop?"

"Worse," he says. "Disco. So—anything from Juilliard?"

"*Nyet*. But Lindsay says I'm a . . . a what?"

"A shoo-in?" he asks.

"*Da*. That's it. A shoo-in"

He laughs. "Lindsay knows all."

The Q train pulls into the station outside my window.

"I'm bored," I tell him, though it's a lie. Bored is not what I am. "My father went out with an old friend from Moscow."

"I'm bored, too," answers Ben.

"I don't know if it's good for Pop. He was just beginning to accept that things are different. He's got a driver's papers you know."

"Yeah. Driver's license. Good thing to have."

"No. I mean a *driver* license. A what-do-you-call-it. Taxi and limousine."

"Ooooh," says Ben. "Got it."

I'm silent, remembering that I had told Pop I would remind Ben about his father, about making some introductions. I didn't. I don't.

"This friend," I begin. "He's . . ."

I can feel Ben waiting. This friend, he's a mooch? A family member? A last hope? A lost cause? A *refusenik*? A Jew? An "uncle?"

"He's an operator."

"What do you mean?"

"I mean we didn't even know he was coming. Even though he's the one who got us here and was supposed to be letting us know about, certain things at home. But now he's here and it's strange—why didn't we know? I mean what if we hadn't . . ." *Slow down Marina,* I'm thinking. *Shut it. Shut it down.* But somehow I can't.

"You don't trust him," says Ben.

"No. Of course I do. He's my Dyadya Gosha. I'm just . . . you know sometimes people talk a lot of . . . bunk," I finish lamely, using an old-fashioned word.

"Jive talking," says Ben in English. "It's called jive talking. The song you like.

"Really?" I ask, though he's just sung it for me in

a barrage of consonants, even in the whispery voice. "That's so funny. But it sounds like a different kind of song."

"Yeah," agrees Ben. "It's not an angry song. Quite the opposite. It's a flirty song. An I-call-bullshit-on-you song."

"You snake," I supply, trying to keep up my end in English.

"Exactly." He pauses. "Actually. It's a pretty excellent song. I have the whole album. On tape."

"You snake," I tease.

"Listen. I'm bored and you're bored and you have a Bee Gees jones and I am swearing you to secrecy when I say that I have a Bee Gees album, so how about I bring you some music," he says.

I'm surprised at my knees, how they suddenly feel drunk.

"Okay," I say.

"Twenty minutes, then."

Only after we hang up do I worry that Pop and Gosha might come home. And that Benjamin Frame will be here to witness it. I decide I don't care. *When there is no one to trust, Marya, you must make everyone believe that you trust only them.*

Bullshit, I think. I call bullshit on you, Gosha.

I start cleaning the remains of dinner from the table, but then I wonder if I'd rather Ben see that I have a real life, a real home, and real food. Instead I rush back to my room to see what sort of impression my real life might make. I pull the covers up on the bed, open the

windows a crack, and stuff a bra into a drawer. There's
not much else to be done. I don't have possessions to
arrange or display. The best I can do is brush my hair,
put on a clean T-shirt. *Be cool.* That's what Lindsay
would advise.

In the hallway I notice the small suitcase that Gosha
has left. It has a lock on it. I think back on his hand
heavy on mine: *Make me believe that you trust me.*

Jive talking.

I grab a knife from the kitchen and bust open the lock.

Inside are a few shirts, two bottles of vodka, a pair of
new shoes—Italian leather—and a thick packet wrapped
in heavy bound paper and tied up with string. Yes, I
open that, too.

The papers are thin, Soviet, cheap. The stamps are
heavy, Soviet, archaic. The documents assert the following:

That Svetlana Dukovskaya has been diagnosed with
advanced schizophrenia and sociopathic anti-state irrep-
arable delusion.

That Svetlana Dukovskaya has been classified as an
"intelligence risk" and as an "enemy of the people."

In short, that Svetlana Dukovskaya has been given a
life sentence.

Which is better than a death sentence.

THESE PAPERS I LEAVE clipped together and on the floor. They
are papers for my father and me, not for Georgi's
suitcase. There are others, too: handwritten notes on
classroom grid paper, the shredded left margin disguising

the impact of the words. I read them through carefully, each passing page becoming more surreal.

Page one details *modified strain of anthracis basillicus . . . refined grade capable of exportation, human smuggling . . . quantities to encompass New York, Philadelphia, Atlanta, Dallas, Chicago, and Los Angeles via aerial coverage . . . super-plague, weaponized.* Notes about a weapons-grade anthrax program, long denied and now scrutinized. And apparently, underway at Lukino.

The second page is a list of names, scientists.

The third page is also covered in Georgi's sloppy handwriting. But it is noted *Dictation.* As I read it, I hear my mother's voice—concise, unwavering, and a touch dramatic:

The destruction of the civilian village of Lukino took place over the weekend of May 26, 1978. It was caused by human exposure to aerosolized anthrax. The rapidity of infection and virulence of re-infection among the population was surprising even to the authorities. The number of victims still hasn't been recorded, because the compound could not handle all the bodies, even after opening the blast chambers to be used as temporary morgues. There was no choice but to allow the municipal hospitals to take in the infected, and on the third day, all the local staff were dismissed and the hospitals left untended. The army—yes Georgi, our soldiers! —were sent to guard the perimeters of the local clinics and hospitals while the people died in agony inside. And the physicians who had witnessed the symptoms during those first 24 hours?

They were sent to camps. They never came back. The alibi focused on consumed anthrax from tainted meat.

But the certainty, Georgi, that no one has ever documented, is that the exposure began as a deliberate experiment. It was a human trial.

This is how I know, Georgi. I know because I saw the children.

First it was orphans. No one notices orphans. But one of them, one of them was chosen in error. She was a young dancer. She was visiting the orphanage with her dance class. Some sort of cultural evening for the poor residents. And that is what I saw, Georgi. I saw her confusion as she was left behind and then transferred with the others and "inoculated." That's what they said. And I saw, in my vision, this ballerina, just fifteen years old. I saw her die in agony. And it was she who told me what happened to her and to the other children and then, when it became entirely out of control, to the whole village of Lukino.

Human exposure to aerosolized anthrax. The rapidity of contagion and contamination surprising even to the authorities. Doctors were sacrificed to the research of our secret defense program, Gosha. Doctors, and administrators—innocents like Vitya. Even a ballerina. A beautiful ballerina is killed for the Motherland. And then it was all covered up . . . But I saw it.

The papers shake in my hands. 1978. The year before my father was transferred to Lukino. It is true. Pop had said she knew more than he ever could. That she could see the past. Gosha had said she told him everything. That she was lucid.

I feel strange. Like I'm in and out of my body. Like I can see forever but am also blind. I feel like Sveta is inside me. And also gone to us. Forever. Through the fog of my thoughts I hear a voice on the radio announce that it is 10:30 P.M. and that coming up next is a live broadcast from Lincoln Center . . .

I stuff the handwritten papers back into their envelope. I'm sliding the whole thing back into Georgi's suitcase, when a small, dog-eared photograph slips from the stash and drops into my lap.

It's a picture of me, riding on Pop's shoulders—laughing my fool head off—as Ma stands nearby, her arms up raised in case I should fall.

I close the suitcase and stand. As I am looking down at this photo—this old shadow of innocence, the picture telescopes and recedes far from my reach until it is no more than a tiny dot floating in the long tunnel of the hallway.

There is a noise behind me and I turn my head, which is too heavy, too slow. The hallway has gone dark. The front door opens on a figure haloed in light. The figure has no features but holds a gun. The figure drifts into the living room and I follow. Except that I don't. I only *see* myself follow, and when I am there, in the presence of this vision, there is a third person there, too. It is my father, and he is lying facedown on the floor.

I hear myself cry out. The figure with the gun turns on me. But instead of a gun, he is holding a book. I reach out, one hand grasping it. The other hand is on my heart. And when I pull both away, they are covered in blood.

And then the darkness lifts.

I am weeping in the hallway. Trembling in the hallway. Crouched in the hallway and Benjamin Frame is holding me, asking me what has happened, what is wrong.

I have had another vision. That's what I tell him.

PART THREE

BRIGHTON BEACH FEBRUARY 1983

MUSIC
TO DIE FOR

NINE
ROMANCE

Lindsay and I are in her bedroom, halfway through a pint of ice cream, when she asks if she can "just please bitch a little here." Lindsay doesn't complain much, but when she does it's a true education. After her last outburst I mastered multiple English expressions of disgust, including "gag me." It came in handy when Fred Berkeley made a lewd suggestion in the cafeteria. Lindsay had high-fived me. Since then I've muttered it under my breath more than once in response to Gosha's cheerful greetings: *Privyet, Sunshine. Let me talk to your Pop . . .*

"By all means," I tell her. "Bitch your heart away."

"Out," she corrects me. "Bitch your heart *out.*" She licks the back of the spoon and hands it to me for a turn at the battered carton. "It's just that he's such an arrogant shithead sometimes."

I wait. The shithead, I know, is Benjamin Frame.

"I mean . . . Do you know Leon Ronkov? Do you? Well Leon is totally into me. Like, totally into me. And has been for a long time. And he asked me to go hear The Romantics with him at Broadway Garage, and so I tell Ben this, right? And used to be that if I said Leon Ronkov asked me out, Ben would go, oh—okay, well I guess I can give him a ride, too. You know what I mean? And it was arrogant but it was kind of cool, the way he would be all assuming. Like I won't go anywhere without him. But this time he just says, you know, I should have a good time."

She pauses again, waiting for me to respond. I can only shrug.

"Get this," she says "He told me he feels 'claustrophobic' at the Garage. Like—what the hell is that? Who gets claustrophobic? Only arrogant shitheads from Juilliard, that's who." Lindsay sniffs and takes the spoon back for another heaping spoonful of mint chocolate chip. "Screw him." Then she adds, "No offense. I mean about Juilliard."

It's been a month since von Schlief called to accept me into the program. Because of my "language deficiencies" and lack of a "corresponding transcript" from my Soviet past, I still attend Bay High every day until two o'clock. Then I'm excused to schlep it to Juilliard. So Lindsay and I still see each other daily.

We've become friends. In fact, at this point, I am almost as close to Lindsay as I once was with Anya. Between Anya and me there was ballet. Between Lindsay and me there is Ben. But maybe that's the

wrong preposition. Maybe not *between*, but *with*. Or
because.

"Well, no, I don't know Leon Ronkov," I say. "But if
he likes to go to Broadway . . ."

"Garage," cues Lindsay. "Broadway Garage."

"Broadway Garage, and Ben does not, then maybe
he's the guy to better spend time with now. Just like I'm
the girl to better spend time with now because I like ice
cream. I'm not arrogant about ice cream."

Lindsay smiles. "Nope. True. You're a real equal
opportunity ice cream fan."

"I think maybe things now are hard for Ben," I say
in his defense. "It's important semester. He's working on
composition for what do you call it? Exit project? He is
just, you know . . . busy in the head."

I know this is true. Ben told me himself. He told me by
way of an apology. Since the night Gosha arrived and I
had the episode—the night when I told Ben some things
and didn't tell him other things—things are different. That
night one wall came down, but another one went up.

It's not a wall, really. It's more like a scrim, a gauze
curtain that we let hang between us. It's not keeping us
apart. It's just a part of the picture that has to be there.
To establish depth. Perspective. Like the columns in
those Renaissance paintings that determine where Plato
and all his students stand. That's me and Ben.

If we pass each other on the plaza at Lincoln Center
or in the Juilliard halls he asks me how I am. I say,
"I'm okay." He raises his eyebrows, like for confirmation, and I say, "Really." We avoid the long subway

ride home together. It's not hard. We are on different schedules. He still calls me some nights, often late, and we talk about music. Not about Lindsay. Not about Pop. Not about my visions. I have become very fluent in music.

So I'm not surprised that Lindsay feels his distance. I feel it, too. And I feel for her. I only just met the guy, really. And though we've had a sort of intense acquaintanceship, I can't say I know him. Not like Lindsay. Not "since, like, forever."

Lindsay puts the ice cream container on her bedside table. Her bed is a nest of tie-dyed sheets, magazines, scribbled song lyrics and discarded garments that confuse me: half lingerie and half commando garb. She groans. "Boys. They're impossible. You're so lucky that you are distracted by other things. More important things."

I don't answer.

I feel safe here in Lindsay's bubble of self, where there is no room for my own concerns. I was here last Sunday, too, letting Lindsay distract me from my father's strange behavior and Gosha's talk. Jive talk.

Gosh has found a flat of his own, or so he says, but he still spends most of his time at our place. Or driving around with Pop. "On meetings," he boasts in English that is less accented than Pop's. When I try to talk to him about the papers I found he either acts like I must have been dreaming ("List of secret labs? *Nyet, dochka*, Sveta was prescient, but she wasn't a database") or he implies that he's turned them all over to Pop already, and I should trust Pop above all.

Pop is drinking a lot. And driving.

I rise and move to the window. Beyond the faded curtains is a nasty sleeting Sheepshead Sunday afternoon. My family problems, unlike Lindsay's woes with Ben, are unlikely to come haunting me here. But even as I tell myself this, out of the blue, Lindsay says:

"Masha says your father is driving some *bratva* heavies around these days. You know about that, Mar?"

I turn and look at her, wondering.

"Yeah, she says that he's always at the wheel of Vova Skilarsky, who's, you know, like a big mafia dude."

You don't know what the fuck you're talking about, Lindsay, I think. But something tells me she does.

"I mean, I'm not passing judgment or anything, Mar. It's totally cool with me. Your dad getting connected? Cuz I totally want to be a fly on the wall at another *bratva* bar mitzvah or something. Masha's cut me off."

"No way," I insist. "It's not like that. No way like that. My father is microbiologist. He has advanced degrees. But, like me, no transcripts, you know? No, how do you say it . . . no *dokazatel'stva,* no proof. No common language, you see? Soviet and American past, present, future. You have to start over. So Pop has to drive for a while. But no. No mafia. Never."

Lindsay offers me a sympathetic smile. "Right. No—I totally get it. Totally. I just am telling you what Masha says, okay? Because the *bratva,* from what I understand, that's not like a 'temporary situation'—know what I mean, Mar? Just be prepared, that's all I'm saying."

She jumps from the bed and cranks the volume on

The Romantics, who are just as enthusiastic and happy and forgiving as she is.

Now she's in the bathroom, rummaging under the sink. "Hooray!" she shouts, one hand brandishing a box of hair dye from around the doorway. Jet black. I oblige.

"Maybe you can talk to Ben, huh, Marina? See if it's just me. Or maybe, I dunno, maybe there's something he's not telling me. It's just so weird—we always used to tell each other everything."

She's swaddled in a stained towel and bent under the tap's warm water. She looks much younger with her hair in a plastic net, blue-black fingers creeping down her forehead. I scrub at her brow, and then smooth away the worry lines.

"Sure," I say.

And I mean it. It's time for me and Ben to step off our ledges. No more David Bowie digressions. No more Eurythmics and existentialism. We'll talk about Lindsay. And . . . whatever it is he's not telling her.

IT'S TWILIGHT WHEN I leave Lindsay's place, though that's a lovelier name than the hour itself.

At the esplanade on the marina, the ravens are bold and raucous. Ben says they are not ravens, but crows. All I know is that they are *voroni*, just like the black guardians of balconies and trash bins in Moscow. They perch on Kremlin walls and on bay-swept benches. I love them and I hate them. Tonight I hate them, but only a little bit. They remind me of a life long ago. And of the night my mother failed to come home.

I walk right through their bravado, welcoming a stare-down. They rarely win, these big black birds that look you in the eye. But they make a god-awful squawk just before they lose, just before you get the better of them.

Across the intersection that brings the roads from Sheepshead Bay and Brighton together, a car is idling. Blue exhaust spills across the street. I slow down, not wanting to walk into its line of sight. Without know-ing for certain, I wait to see. Is it my father idling? Waiting for his mafia fare?

In fact, it's not Pop at the wheel. No. Pop's in the back seat. And now he's emerged from the car. Now he's hunched over against the sleet, walking away from the car. I've got four lanes of traffic between me and him, but I dart across them all against the light. When I'm on the far side, I hold my umbrella across my face and pass the car. I can't see into the darkened windows.

I hurry up the side street where Pop has disappeared. He's nowhere in sight. But I know where he is. Halfway up the block a sign hangs over the street advertising the operating hours of *Russkaya Banya*. A cloud of euca-lyptus and steam escapes from an open window. Pop's taking a *shvitz*. It's that simple. Nothing treacherous, no hidden agenda.

I stand on the sidewalk outside the bathhouse and wonder why it doesn't feel simple. Pop was empty-handed. He was alone. He came in a strange car with tinted windows.

I wait for a long time, watching the men entering, identical in quilted coats and worn pants, clutching plastic bags that I know carry soap, sandals, nail clippers, and a bottle of vodka. I watch them exit, louder now, and in pairs. Red-faced and brave. Clean. A little drunk. Refreshed. A little more content with their American exile, where the steam is not quite as smoky as at home, the birch not quite as green as at home, but the *banya* still braces you against February sleet—just like at home.

The door opens and releases a different type. Five men in leather coats, shiny pants, uninterested in the sleet, unimpressed with the sauna. Not a plastic bag among them. Pistols don't get carried in plastic bags.

Thieves of the law. *Vori v'zakone.*

Not to be confused with *voroni,* though. No. I won't be staring these shifty, squawky creatures down. Not even that one in the back, the only one whose face still retains a spark of intelligence.

Dyadya Gosha.

Now the door opens once more and my father steps out. I duck farther into the shadows and watch as the raven-black car with tinted windows pulls up in front of the *banya* and all the men pile in. All except Pop. He just says, *"Nu da, davay."* Okay, then. Later.

Then he turns and walks into the sleet alone.

I watch my father disappear once again into the wet night and remember something else that Ben told me about the *voroni.*

"You know what you call a bunch of crows together? It's called a 'murder.' A murder of crows."

• • •

I'VE BEEN HOME FOR hours by the time Pop arrives, smelling of the street, of smoke, of secrets. He kisses me on the head and starts pulling out the couch. "I'm tired, Marya," he says. "Let me sleep."

"I need to talk to you. Really."

"I have a long day tomorrow, Marya. Can't it wait?"

I consider.

"Why a long day?" I ask. "What will you do? Drive a car? Wait in a back lot? Or do you have a meeting? A date with your new pals down at the Corsair?"

He eyes me. Knows I am accusing him. The Corsair is Vova Skilarsky's nightclub: pole dancers and thugs; Lindsay's notion of the mafia. It's just catty-corner from our apartment. I pass it daily on my way from school.

"For your information, Miss Interrogator, I have an appointment with some important people at Stony Brook."

"What's that?"

"Stony Brook lab. Most prestigious research lab in New York. I have a meeting with some of the directors."

"*Da?* Really?" I ask. "Pop—that's great! Is there a job?"

"Oy, Marya. Job, shmob. There's only opportunities and what we make of them, right? Did I ask you when you went to Lincoln Center if there was a vacancy? No. There is only what you have. What I know. There is only this."

Pop has pulled the sofa out and is struggling with the American sheets that, because of their odd elastic corners, will never lie straight on the bed. I help him out. Now he takes off his pants, folds them neatly on the chair. His shirt he tosses to me. I am in charge of the laundromat. He climbs underneath the covers and switches off the lamp. The mattress heaves. He sighs and says, "I promised you, Marina. Things will be right. I will bring her home. I will move us out of this ghetto. I will have a proper goddamn bed with proper goddamn sheets."

I stand in the dark until he begins to snore.

Then I make my way to my own room, The Romantics needling me, whispering in my ear, telling me things I don't want to hear.

"LINDSAY IS WORRIED ABOUT you. She thinks you are being, what's the word, 'distant,'" I say, choosing a milder synonym for the "arrogant" that Lindsay had thrown around. "She thinks you are giving her the cold shoulder."

Ben and I are sitting in the café across the street from Juilliard, two of us in a sea of talent, ambition, violin cases, and denim jackets.

He frowns slightly. "Really? That's what you wanted to talk about?"

I shrug. "I thought maybe you should know."

"Yeah, Marya, I know," he replies. "She's right. I am. I'm giving her some space. She needs to do her own thing right now. I love Linds, I do, but she thinks she needs me more than she does. I don't want to be the big brother forever, you know?"

"I don't think that Lindsay wants you to be her big brother, either," I say. Then I wish I hadn't. "It's not my business. Sorry."

"It's all right," says Ben. There's a silence as he regards

me. "She's lucky to have you as a friend." For a minute I think he's embarrassed, but then he laughs. "But if she thinks I'm going to go hear those pansies in their pink suits . . ." He shakes his head. "You know The Romantics, right?"

I nod. Four boys, big hair, skinny ties, patent leather. Infectious beat. Fun lyrics. Lindsay had hugged me when I told her, "I dig The Romantics."

But Ben puts on a simpering voice, bugs his eyes out and starts bobbing his head idiotically. In fact, he does a pretty good "pretty boy," with his bouncing curls and dancing brown eyes. Now he's pretending to play drums that aren't there, and though I know he trying to look like a jackass, in fact Ben looks like a talented drummer who has lost his drum.

"*Baby hold me tight. You feel so right. You have an overbite. You don't know how to fight.*"

"That's not how it goes," I correct him. "It goes like this: *I like you because you know how to dance, and you are like romance, and you jump up and down and . . .*" I'm doing a pretty good approximation of The Romantics explaining, "What I like About You," but I stumble at the invitation. The come-on. The part where I sing that he's the only one, and does he want to come over tonight?

Ben has stopped drumming. He's watching me, the smallest of smiles on his face.

"Yup. That's how it goes; you're right," he says.

I hum a bit more, wind it down. Embarrassed, but not apologetic about what I like. I finish the lemonade in my glass and shrug. "I like the song. It's very Beatles."

"Yeah. I guess we'll have to agree to disagree on this one." He looks away. "Maybe you can go with Lindsay and what's-his-name. The Garage is a good club."

It seems like a dismissal. I stand to go, but Ben puts his hand on my arm. "Sit a second."

I do.

"Marya. Tell me what that vision meant to you. Your dad."

I look around at the café, full of chattering kids. I remember when this was a daydream: Marina in leg warmers at the cafés of Lincoln Center. It was so long ago—but now it is real. What does any of this mean? I wonder. The things I see. Am I prophetic? No one else dreams their father dead on the floor. Their mother behind bars. No one does that. This isn't a ballerina thing. My dad's words about Sveta's "gift" come back to me.

"I have visions," I start. "Of people I know. Not strangers. I saw my mother as an old woman. I saw my father bleeding."

Ben waits.

"Sometimes I think I might be seeing what might happen. But I can't think too much about the future." I'm explaining slowly, trying to get it right. "Because I don't know what happened in the past."

I feel a lump in my chest. It runs up against my words, and I choke when I say, "Ben, I don't know what has happened to my mother."

He takes my hand. Holds it in his. Says nothing.

"So how can I believe what I see is what might be?" I

ask. "What good is seeing the future when I'm blind to the past?"

I take a deep breath. He had asked. And I'm still fighting tears, because I am thinking of my mother, who I know now had the opposite problem. The past was wide open to her. The past in all its horror cost her the future she couldn't see.

"I do know this," I add, once I've collected myself. "I know that my father is, maybe, making bad decisions."

"I've asked him, several times—*my* dad," says Ben. "I've asked him to look into getting something, you know, legitimate for your father. But I have to tell you, Marya. He can't help if your dad keeps consorting with . . ."

"I know," I interrupt. "I know he's been driving the mafia guy around, but that's just, you know, rent. For God's sake, Ben. We have to live."

There's a long pause. Ben lets go of my hand and rubs his nose, thinking.

"Pop is going to be all right," I say, mostly to myself. "He's been on several interviews, and he's at Stony Brook today. I mean, if your father can just, you know, mention him. What do you call it. Character reference. Legitimacy."

"That's just it. Your father is already using all his cred. He is going to these places and asking to meet with top-level people. But Marya, it's not right. My father says there's no way he could get access to those people without . . . He's digging in places he shouldn't. He's asking questions that make people very suspicious, and he's using my father's name too freely. It's causing a problem."

My hand is still warm, damp.

"Stony Brook is no Juilliard," he says. "Your dad is overstepping."

"He's Soviet. He doesn't know American protocol . . ."

"That's not it. This isn't about niceties. This isn't about my father's reputation. Although, trust me, he is plenty ready to defend that."

There's a shriek of laughter next to us as a kid in silky harem pants moonwalks his way into a full bin of dirty coffee cups.

Ben doesn't even glance away. He leans closer. "This is about your safety."

I'M LATE FOR MY next class. The instructor gives me what Lindsay calls "the hairy eyeball." It's only fifty minutes of Balanchine technique. For a Bolshoi-trained dancer, that's about as superfluous as a class in "walking around with perfect turn-out and a snooty look on your face." My mind wanders.

Benjamin Frame is worried about my safety.

Where to start? He's right? He's wrong? He is my protector? He's my big brother?

I remember that first night—New Year's Eve. How Ben had turned, left his friends to come to my side. I remember how humiliated I had felt next to those Americans who needed no social rescuing.

I love Linds, I do, Ben had said. And then he basically said, *but she can take care of herself.* Does he think that

I can't take care of myself? Well, isn't he right? And if I could, would Ben respect me more? Or would he just send me off to Broadway Garage with my little friends so he can be left in peace with his musical genius?

I fall off my point and curse: *Blin.*

Eyebrows are raised in my direction.

What am I thinking? Pop is in over his head. Gosha is already at sea. The two of them together sitting on some Cold War heat. Jive talking. And add to this what Ben doesn't even know. That all this time I'm planted stage-right, just waiting for somebody's spotlight: *Hello hello, what have we here, a talented teenage ballerina bearing a striking resemblance to one recent enemy of the state?* Absolutely nothing is under control here. Things are going to derail. I've been warned. By my own extra-sensitive mind. And here I am fretting over what Benjamin Frame thinks?

Gospodi, Marina. Get yourself together.

I decide to start now. I will focus. Pushing everything from my head I concentrate on the music. Four/four, *lentamente*, the coda giving me eight bars to expand, fill the floor with my body, with perfectly formed lines. Here I begin. Here I end. All is visible. Chin in line with shoulder in line with hip in line with knee. My arch measurable with a protractor. Calculated and known. Poise. Control. Presence. Present.

"Very nice, Marina," says von Schlief. I didn't even see her enter.

After class she asks me to stay behind.

"Marina, I thought you would be pleased to know

that you have been selected to workshop a new étude over at ABT," she says.

"At American Ballet?"

"Indeed. You'll join the second corps, and we'd like to partner you with one of their junior principals who has just arrived. He's catching up, and they think it will go easier for him with a Russian-trained intermediate. Like you. Right size and body type, too."

Von Schlief folds her arms over her chest. There's a glint in her eye, but I'm not sure what it means. I remember my father and his certainty that I am practicing to be a pawn of the American Ballet. A pawn in search of a missing Queen.

She spins and walks to the door, opens it and calls down the hallway: "Please join us, Sergei."

He's Russian. Broad shouldered. Sculptured chest. He moves like a cat. But this one is a cat that, maybe, can also swim rapids or scale rock walls. He certainly can land on his feet. And catch me at the same time. Yikes. All of my focus is shattered. I feel vertigo.

He nods to von Schlief, crosses the room and takes my hand. Kisses it. What is this? Nobody does that. Certainly not a Soviet dancer who can't be older than twenty.

"*Enchanté*," he says.

Please, I think. As in: *Yes, please.*

"Sergei has been dancing with the San Francisco Ballet for the past five years," says von Schlief. "He joined ABT last month. From where originally, Sergei? In Russia?"

"Rostov," he says. His eyes have not left mine. They are grey. Direct.

"Ah, yes," she says breezily. "Cossacks and all that. All right then, let's see how you two do together. Let's have paired arabesques *en devant* followed by *bourree relevés* and reverse through *en face*. Then we'll see some lifts and turns."

For the next twenty minutes San-Francisco-Sergei-from-Rostov models my form on his own. He lifts my leg higher, turns my extension tighter, stretches my lines longer, and holds my balance steadier. I can feel von Schlief seeing his mastery and my malleability. I'm breathing hard and we haven't even begun moving. But he is in control.

Make everyone believe that you trust only them.

Right you are, Gosha. I can do that, I think, as this boy with eyes the color of the River Don barges into my den of paranoia, lifts me to his shoulder, and promenades me in a circle that I know will end with my perfect swan dive to within an inch of the floor. To kiss his feet. Because when he dances with me I am the old Marina. The one who is at home, a queen on the stage, her prince a broad-shouldered *bogatyr* from Rostov.

The Romantics and their silly love songs are banished from my mind. This boy really knows how to dance.

TEN
SPEAKEASY

It's the Sunday before Valentine's Day when Lindsay reveals her perfect alternative plan to "roses and candy and excessive PDA."

"PDA?" I ask. I glance at Ben. He stares at his feet.

"Public Display of Affection," she clarifies. "Not cool."

All week, she has been assuring me there's nothing lamer than a Valentine's Dance at Bay High School.

"Believe me. I've been to my share," she insisted.

I didn't argue. Even if, secretly, I have my own fantasy about going to the dance with a certain junior principal from Rostov, and it is not even a little bit lame. Besides, Lindsay knows about Sergei, this guy that I've only just met but who has already asked if he could take me out next Saturday.

"Jesus, Marya. He asks you out for a first date on Valentine's Day?" she marveled.

Pop, on the other hand, displayed no surprise at all. On the contrary, he had a perfectly insane explanation for Sergei's forwardness.

"He's the one, Marina," he said. "That's who they've sent."

And then he had described to me how "Sergei" was our "contact." How he would "intercede with the KGB" on behalf of Sveta. How Pop just needed a little more time to "collect all the information," and then he would hand it over. How Sergei would handle it from there. How Sveta would be "released on exchange." How I just had to make sure not to "blow this," but needed to bring Sergei to him "discreetly."

I am the one putting air quotes on Pop's crazy ideas. Because they are crazy. Right? Aren't they crazy?

Still, it was Lindsay who insisted that I turn my date with Sergei into a double date. "And don't even think of bringing him out to Brooklyn," she had said. "This year we're doing V-Day in the city."

By "the city," Lindsay means Manhattan. Or, more specifically, the Village. The Village is the only part of "the city" that counts. And not the West Village, no. The West Village, with its record stores and jazz clubs and coffee houses, is for girls with feathered hair and colorful mittens. Lindsay's village is the East Village— for girls with bruises wearing too much makeup.

So she has summoned Ben and me to her place to hear her perfect plan. We arrived at her door at the same time and exchanged our usual public greeting.

"How are you?"

"I'm good. How are you?"

"You know . . ."

Once upstairs, Lindsay has become a whirl of activity. "You are going to love this," she says, pulling a long box from under her bed. "Well, I mean Marya's going to love this. Ben, you are just going to have to endure it and be nice. That's your job this year. I won't make you go to a Valentine's Day dance and you . . . you are going to humor me."

She opens the lid, smiling mischievously. Then she tosses a hat at me. It's one of those movie hats. Like the men wear in black-and-white, when they spend the whole film putting out cigarettes without smoking them and running up and down the hills of San Francisco with pistols in their hands.

I try it on. Lindsay leans over and tilts it.

"Gangster-style," she says, placing a similar hat on her own head.

Next she pulls out a two-foot-long gun. Honest. It's like in the movies, too. With two handle grips and a ribbed barrel and a round clip as big as a shot-putt. Plastic, of course. I laugh out loud as she mugs.

"Tommy gun," I say, wondering how I know that.

"That's right, sister," she confirms. "We're going to a Valentine's Day Massacre."

I don't know that word.

"Oh, it's legendary. Historic, I mean," explains Lindsay. "So in nineteen twenty-nine, there's this mafia war in, I dunno, Chicago maybe and basically these mobsters just rub out the entire rival—"

Ben interrupts. "A dress-up party, Linds? I'd think you'd be the first to see through that baloney. You really want to spend the night in some Al Capone theme park?"

But Lindsay is wily. "Suit yourself. You don't have to come, Ben. Though it's a shame. I mean, you'd rip it up in a pinstripe suit and suspenders. Like Warren Beatty in *Bonnie and Clyde*. Plus, get this—it's this new club, Lansky's. They're calling it a 'speakeasy.' So you know there's gonna be a raid, and we'll all have to run out the back door, and you probably won't even have to stay more than forty-five minutes, tops."

Ben glances at me.

"She's right," I say. "I mean about Warren Beatty." My cheeks are suddenly warm. I turn away.

"C'mon, Ben. Marya already has a date. You're not gonna make me the third wheel are you? Make me the damn getaway driver."

Lindsay is adjusting the fedora in the mirror, applying lipstick. But Ben is still looking at me.

"Who are you going with?" he asks softly.

"Dancer. He's a dancer. Named Sergei. Just. A dancer."

"English, please," commands Lindsay.

"I dunno, Linds," says Ben. "I'll let you know tonight." He picks up the fake gun, tosses it back down on the bed. Stuffs his hands in his pockets. Sits down. Stands up. "I mean, never mind, screw it. I'll go. If it's 'speakeasy' they're after, there should be some decent jazz, right?"

Lindsay throws her arms around him and plants a big kiss on his cheek. "Killer! Yay, Ben! Hey, remember last

year? How awful the dance was? How I was an idiot
about the corsage and we left after two songs because
you said you wouldn't stay in the same room as Lionel
Richie?"

She grins at me. "We played pool all night instead.
But this is going to be so much cooler. I'm going to be
so badass. But Marina—you need to go glamorous.
Haughty and screen star. A, what's it called?—a gangster moll."

"Hey, don't start with the 'mafia rocks' crap, okay?"
Ben's got an edge in his voice. "I mean, I get the attrac-
tion, the era, the flapper stuff, but you've got to ease
up on your criminal fetish, Linds. It's not cool. It's not
awesome."

I look at him. He's messing with the toy gun again.
For the first time I realize what he sees. Teenage girls
romanticizing the mafia. One thing for Lindsay and
her *bratva* infatuation. Quite another thing for me
and my *bratva* liability. I see it dawn on Lindsay, too.

"Shit. I didn't mean . . ." She glances at me.

My heart flips and then sinks like a rock. I can handle
this. There are so many ways I can handle this. I can be
outraged. I can be philosophical. I can shrug it off. I go for
sarcasm: "I think maybe instead of suspenders, Ben, I can
give you track suit and driver's cap from my dad. Maybe
also leather jacket. You know, kind that look tough only
if you are in Kharkov or Brighton Beach. Lindsay and I
will be Hollywood. You will be . . . authentic."

It's not funny. The room is heavy. Silent. Awkward.
Hurt.

"Let's skip it," says Lindsay finally. "Let's just go play pool instead."

"No," answers Ben. "Marya's right. No need to confuse playacting with reality." He rises from the bed. "I gotta go."

On his way to the door he stops next to me. "I'm sorry," he says. I just nod. Tuck my hair behind my ear. I am, too.

"Your English has gotten very good," he adds. Then he leaves.

SO WE ARE GOING to this Lansky's. On a double date. Me and Lindsay are standing on her porch in our pin curls and red lipstick when Ben pulls up in a cab. He hops out and opens the rear door with a flourish.

"Ladies," he says.

Benjamin Frame has risen to the occasion. He's not just wearing a Jazz Age suit; he's affected a Jazz Age swagger. He crosses one well-shod foot over the other, tugs the brim of his hat down low, adjusts the knot of his tie.

Benjamin Frame: handsome devil.

Lindsay just turns to me and mouths silently, *ohmygod*.

In the cab he sits between us, allowing Lindsay to paw at him, fuss with his handkerchief, jabber about bathtub gin.

"You be careful now, dollface," he hams in his best Brooklyn accent. "That stuff will go straight to yer pretty head. Next ting you know, I'll have to dance wit my gal slung over my shoulder like a suit bag."

Lindsay giggles, puts a finger to her cheek, and says, "Boop-Oop-a-Doop."

And then Ben starts to riff. Rap. Jive talk. Whatever it is.

It's *scap scap doo be* and *la la be dooby* and *shooby de ska ska* and it's his knee bouncing there in its pin stripes and his slim wrists popping out of his French cuffs, reaching for keys that aren't there but are somewhere in the back of his tongue going *de plink plink doobee.*

"Scat," says Ben. I realize I am gaping at him, openmouthed. "Makes you speak easy."

I couldn't possibly repeat it, his off-the-cuff chorus, but soon it develops words that go something like:

"Goin to the Village goin straight to the Village goin down to the Village to commit a massacre. Gonna waste all the wannabes rubout all the Romeos ruin all the romance and put it on a Ritz. Goin' down to the Village gonna love up all of Lansky's goin' down to the Village to commit a massacre . . ."

It's Ben's tribute to this moment that is the three of us headed into Manhattan together, our own private Valentine.

Lindsay adds a chorus about leaving behind the tommy guns and getting home by curfew. Not such a "badass" after all.

We fly across the bridge, laughing and bragging. When we pull up six blocks later to a fancy-dressed crowd behind a velvet rope, I'm happier than I have been since . . . since when?

And then I see Sergei standing by himself, his gabardine coat open to the wind. He, too, looks like a million bucks. Better than Warren Beatty in *Bonnie and Clyde*. But for just a moment I wish him a million miles away. I'm a little scared of our troika becoming a foursome.

I'm the first one out of the cab. Sergei sees me and strides toward us, a dancer's stride. Behind me, I can feel Ben watching. I feel his music die, his rhythm freeze in the frosty air. I hear Lindsay yell, "Yo! Date-man! Wait up!" and I know that Ben's high spirits have given way to something else. I spin on my heel and put one hand on his sleeve.

"*Smotri . . .*" I say. Be nice.

I don't know whether I mean that he should be nice to Sergei or to Lindsay. Or why I should need to ask it.

Ben bristles under his brilliantine.

"*Dobriy vecher.*" Sergei, who is no taller than Ben but holds himself higher, proffers a masculine handshake.

"Hey," is Ben's monosyllabic response. Lindsay catches up with us, lays eyes on Sergei and purrs, "Well, hello, Gary Cooper."

Our massacre has only just begun.

LANSKY'S IS A BASEMENT joint, thick with smoke and red velvet. The tabletops are sticky. The bartender looks like a cross between Boy George and Joan Crawford. I guess if a speakeasy is supposed to be a high-class dive, then Lansky's has succeeded.

Ben gets us a table close to the band, a live orchestra with plenty of horns and snares. He spends the next several minutes engrossed in the sheets of music on the stand nearest us, while Lindsay and I exchange whispers, and Sergei and I cross glances.

I've had exactly two conversations with my date. The first one was after we'd already conducted a pretty thorough non-vocal conversation under von Schlief's steely gaze. The second consisted of real words. He walked me to the subway and let two or three trains pass as he praised my technique before I said, "This one is an express. I really should be getting home."

"Of course," he had said, with an exaggerated bow. "I'll see you . . ." And somehow, what followed was "Saturday?"

And now here we are.

He sits next to me, his knee just centimeters from mine. But it's like I don't recognize him, dressed and dandy and conversational. I can smell his cologne. It throws me off, distracts me from the memory of his hands rotating my waist, the sound of his breathing as he releases me. When we are alone in the studio, Sergei makes me forget the strange situation I am in. But now he has created a new one.

We are drinking gin, just as Lindsay had hoped, and in walks a man with a whisper mustache and a basket of flowers. Sergei doesn't miss a beat and now I am in possession of three red roses. And a wink. A grey-eyed wink. Sergei asks Lindsay how she likes her drink, and she gives it a long and indulgent review.

Now he scoots his chair closer to Ben. He's asking him a question. Juilliard? Ben answers: musical composition.

Sergei follows this with another, but the band has begun and I can't hear what they are saying. I watch their lips form English, then Russian; questions, then answers. Then there seem to be no more questions. Just assertions. Markings of lines and parameters. Sergei's lips are tight. Ben is biting his. He won't meet my gaze.

When the third song begins, Sergei asks me to dance, and though I have no practice negotiating this maniacal American music, I accept. He takes my hand, leads me to the floor. The moment he places his other hand on the small of my back, I am dancing. It's more than form, more than a partner's intuition, more than strength. There is something in his hold that is more than controlling. But before I can decide whether it is too much—Sergei's mastery of me—the crowd has cleared a ring around us. We have become a spectacle.

I won't lie. It is thrilling. Sergei and I are classically trained, so it isn't like the show we put on is quite right for this pseudo-speakeasy in the East Village. But whatever it is, it is enough to alter the course of the night. Because as we are heading back to our seats, a fat man with jowls and a sweat-stained shirt lurches in front of us. He holds an old-fashioned microphone to my face and asks for our names. Then he turns to the room and announces: "Ladies and gentlemen, welcome Sergei and Marina, our first occupants of Murderer's Row!"

With that, we find ourselves sitting on a raised platform clear across the dance floor. I watch Lindsay and Ben react to this turn of events. I see Lindsay insert two fingers into her fire engine lips and deliver a piercing whistle. She's laughing and nudging Ben, but his smile is slippery in the shifting light.

"Well then," whispers Sergei in my ear, "I think they've marked us for execution."

I shoot him a question mark, confused without his hand on my back.

"You know, Valentine's Day Massacre? Seven gangsters dead in a garage?" He makes a show of counting chairs in our new VIP section. "I guess this is what happens when you dance too well." Then he leans in closer and adds, "Or, you know, if you work for the wrong crew."

The music is marvelous, the dance floor is full, and my date is the object of every woman's gaze. The Master of Ceremonies has asked us to remain seated. We will be selecting the next couple to join us on the platform. I let Sergei's comment ride.

At the end of the next song, he and I consult and choose an enthusiastic pair flushed red from their acrobatic exertions on the dance floor. In turn, they select a third couple. Older, venerable, even regal in their period costumes. They share the same silver hair and heavy black makeup. I imagine Lindsay's approval: senior citizen rockers. I crane my neck to find her. She's still at our table, her pretty painted face propped on both hands, her pumps tapping. I wave and she waves back. I can't make out Ben next to her. He is out of the lights.

The sweat-shiny Master of Ceremonies ushers the last couple to our raised table with bonhomie. "No surprises here, ladies and gents. The legendary Chita and Charles will take their places on the massacre masthead! Which, of course, is to be expected when you are looking for some 'usual suspects.' Now as you can see, we've got just one seat left. That's the seat reserved for the sole survivor of the Valentine's Day Massacre. You know the story. One man was pulled live from the slaughter and . . . well, we'll get to that. Now, our own lovely Damsel of Death, Miss Millicent Riviera, has been making the rounds with an eye . . . well, let's just say with an eye."

The crowd cheers as a young woman in a tight red dress vamps into the spotlight. She wiggles her shapely rear and draws a single index finger across her slim neck. The audience laughs approvingly.

"Millicent, my dear, Millicent, who have you chosen and why?" asks the emcee.

The crowd claps louder as Millicent Riviera extends her forearm into the corner and points. I know who she has chosen. The crowd falls quiet so she can tell us why.

"Oh, Maestro," she rasps huskily. "Just look at the love in those sad eyes. That's some love that wants to lay waste to Lansky's."

Millicent Riviera, Damsel of Death, leads Ben by the elbow to the platform and seats him in the chair next to me. He pulls his hat lower over his eyes and shakes his head, like he's fundamentally opposed. Sergei reaches across me to pat him on the shoulder. I see Ben flinch. I look out to find Lindsay, but the floor lights blind me.

"Ladies and gentlemen, Murderer's Row is filled. And after this short break, our band will commence our own special brand of Musical Chairs. So grab a fresh round, and we'll be back in ten for the Musical Massacre."

And just like that, the magic is over. Recorded music fills the room. The band steps toward the bar. The stage lights dim. I jump from the table and hurry across to Lindsay, but she's already risen and is headed toward the back of the club. I catch up with her in the bathroom.

"Oh please, Marya, it's no biggie," she insists. "I mean it's kind of hilarious. Ben's gonna be really pissed at me because he's gotta be a monkey up there. Probably, yeah, that's what will happen." She pulls out her lipstick and takes off the cap. "Mother," she grumbles. The point is smashed and encased in what looks like pencil shavings. "I'm such a makeup retard."

"Come on," I say. "You're coming to Murderer's Row or whatever in hell they call it."

"Waddayamean?"

"This was your idea. You are playing this game, and I'm going to sit in the corner and get drunk. Don't argue with me."

She doesn't. And five minutes later, Lindsay is perched happily above the dance floor between Sergei and Benjamin. Millicent Riviera doesn't notice the switch or doesn't much care. She is back center stage, wiggling her butt and waving a conductor's baton. With a flourish, she starts up the band, and the audience applauds. After a few bars, she leaps up onto the platform and organizes a conga line of all seven of her contestants.

"Ladies and gentlemen!"

The fat man is back at his microphone and mopping his brow. "The Lansky Lounge gives you . . . Musical

Massacre. A round of applause for our contestants. The rules are simple. When the music stops, don't drop."

A short black man in a tuxedo appears from the wings, delivering a martini glass. The Master of Ceremonies raises it, toasting the room.

"For those who are about to swing," he adds with a chuckle, "we serenade you."

He downs his drink and the music swells.

Millicent has Ben by the shoulders now, dancing something my mother used to call the Jitterbug. Sergei is partnered with the "legendary" Chita, and Lindsay is being swung by the flushed swing dancer.

Suddenly there is a cymbal crash. The music stops and a giant red heart, as big as a chandelier, drops from the ceiling directly onto silver-haired Charles. He's on the floor, laughing and unhurt after being felled by a styrofoam Valentine. Millicent rushes over and traces his body in chalk.

"That's one!" she shouts, and the band strikes up again.

The game continues: Millicent and the fat man taking turns with the conductor's wand and the police chalk, the diminishing dancers pairing up haphazardly. After each round and each dropped Valentine, there is one more chalk outline on the floor and one less dancer.

Only Lindsay, Sergei, Ben and the man who isn't Charles are left when the emcee announces: "There are just four murders to go in our Musical Massacre. It's time to remind our players what's at stake. The sole survivor, the only man (or woman) to step from the bloody garage of the Valentine's Day Massacre, will be treated for his wounds, oh yes. Nursed back to health . . . with a bottle of champagne. On the house, ladies and gentlemen! And there's more . . . if the survivor can correctly repeat the actual words of that lucky man when he was questioned by the police that February night in nineteen twenty-nine, he will receive . . ."

The crowd is clapping. Eager to hear.

"He will receive . . ."

More clapping and whistling. Millicent wiggles into the spotlight, whispers in the fat man's ear.

"Oh," says the fat man, giving Millicent a lascivious once-over. "Well that *is* a nice prize."

The crowd whoops and Millicent cues the band. This time, the lights go out. In the darkness, there is nothing visible but the fat man himself as he stands in the center of the stage, crooning the opening lines in a deep baritone:

"Take your cue and come forward. Take a seat where murder sits . . ."

These are the last words I hear, for even as he continues to sing, my ears have gone deaf. My eyes have become heavy. I know I am seeing something that hasn't yet happened when the spotlight shoots wildly through the club like a chased rabbit, landing first on a man with a gun; then on Lindsay's terrified face; and then on the dance floor. I see one of the chalk outlines rise and walk off the stage. There is a crack. A cymbal. Total blackness. I hear Dyadya Gosha's voice saying, "*Who do you trust, dochka?*" And then the utter darkness is broken by a spotlight: steady, small, and centered on the face of

Benjamin Frame, who pronounces clearly: "*I ain't sayin nothing.*"

"That is correct! Ladies and gentleman, our winner!"

The club is full of laughter and light, and I am staring at my thighs, at the dark wet stain that is spreading across my dress. The glass is still in my lap, and as I jerk upright, it falls to the floor and shatters. I feel as if I am moving in slow motion as I reach across the table for a napkin to wipe my arm, my lap, my parched lips.

Suddenly Ben is kneeling beside me.

"You're pale. You're . . . what happened?" he asks.

"I think I blacked out," I say.

"Come on," he says. "Outside."

"Your prize, lucky survivor," I hear dimly behind me as Ben ushers me through a formless crowd.

We're on the street, but I am sweating in the cold wind. Ben takes off his jacket and drapes it over my shoulders, guiding me to a nearby bench.

"What happened?" he asks.

"It happened," I say.

We sit like that, saying no more. Our silence is broken by Lindsay's excited voice.

"Oh my God, Ben. How did you know the answer? Huh? Who knew you were such a gangster trivia master? Did you hear that, Marya? So apparently they shot this guy up all to pieces but he doesn't die and in the hospital when they asked him what happened he just says—"

"Jesus, Lindsay," says Ben. "Could you just put a sock in it for two minutes maybe?"

I look up, my head lolling under its own weight. Lindsay and Sergei have joined us on the sidewalk. I see confusion in Lindsay's face, turning into concern. But not Sergei. Sergei looks like a man with business to attend to. He says, "I'll take Marina home. My car is around the corner. You two should stay. Enjoy your prize." He's holding aloft an enormous magnum of champagne.

"Uh, no." says Ben. His voice has that edge again. "We live way the hell out in Brooklyn. It's fine. We'll take a cab. Lindsay and I will get her home."

"What's going on?" asks Lindsay. "Marya, you drink too much sweetie?" She crouches down, shivering, and takes my hand.

"No," I say. The memory of her frightened face flashes before me, and is gone. "Well, maybe."

Ben and Sergei have walked away from us, their backs turned, their words hushed. I watch them argue: two discreet Russians. Lindsay is watching, too. I see that her hair has come undone. Her stocking is ripped. I'm struck with the sad thought that I've ruined her night, spoiled all her fun. The champagne bottle is on the ground, forgotten.

Sergei turns and shouts. "Marina, I'm getting the car. I'll pick you up here." I hear this but can't react. Pick me up. Here. Like the forgotten champagne.

Ben comes back to where we are sitting. He pulls his wallet from his pocket and thrusts bills in Lindsay's hand. "Settle up and get the coats," he says, jerking her up and pushing her back to the club. It is nasty.

Unnecessary. So . . . arrogant. Lindsay looks at him for a moment then just shakes her head.

"I'm sorry, Lindsay," I say as she walks back in the club. But I'm not the one who should apologize, even if I did just sabotage the night. I look at Ben. "What's wrong with you?"

"I think we should just get a cab and go. Get the hell out of here."

"What's *wrong* with you?" I ask again, in Russian, and this time he hears me. "Why did you have to treat Lindsay like that?"

"At least she listens to me," Ben snaps. "At least she trusts me. I know what I'm talking about, Marya. I know what I'm talking about here."

"What are you talking about here, Ben?"

He takes his hat off, throws it on the ground.

"I don't like that guy."

I snort.

"Oh you don't, huh? Well I don't think he likes you so much either. Not that you've made any attempt to be likable tonight."

I'm not sure how mad I am. Or why. All I know is that Ben is trying to shut a door, and I haven't figured out what's behind it. It's a door that my father wants open. I know it's crazy, but . . . I glance down the street. Sergei is gone, vanished around the corner or maybe forever. And now I do want to go with him. As far as he is going. Maybe to Rostov. Maybe to bed. I don't know, but I want him.

"I don't trust him," says Ben. It sounds stupid.

"Oh, you don't trust him? Well, maybe I do. Maybe

he's someone who can help me in ways you can't. You know?" My voice is too shrill, even to my own ears. "You have no idea who he is."

"Who he is?" he asks. Now he is incredulous. "Who he is? Marya, who the hell do *you* think he is?"

I can't say it. I can't admit it. I'm embarrassed. Also confused. So I blurt out something equally stupid. I turn it all upside down.

"What? Do you think he's a spy or something, Ben? Because my father thinks he's a spy."

And then I laugh like a maniac.

SERGEI DRIVES ME HOME. Alone. Ben didn't even say goodbye. He would have nothing to do with me after what I said. It still hurts my ears: "*Someone who can help me in ways you can't.*"

Sergei is calm, in control as always, navigating the night traffic of the expressway. I watch his profile, crossed and criss-crossed with headlights. I want to touch his face. I want to make him tear his eyes from the road. I want to know why Ben called him what he did. Why he said with so much scorn, "No, Marya. I don't think he's a spy. I think he's a douche."

"*Shto takoe 'dush?'*" I ask now.

"Dush?" Sergei repeats, "What do you mean? *Dush* is 'shower' in English. *Da*, 'shower.' Why? Feeling sticky from that gin fizz you spilled on your dress?"

I shake my head. I'm pretty sure that's not what Ben meant.

"So your pal Ben, he's a jazzman?"

I nod but mentally correct him: *a piano man.*

"His father, too? A musical family?"

"No. His dad's a . . ." I don't know why I hesitate, but I do. Maybe it's a concession to Ben and his distrust. Or maybe I just don't want to talk about chemistry. I'd rather feel it.

"Ben's the only musician."

Sergei nods. "Can't say I'm a huge fan of that American jazz. All that gibberish singing."

"It's called scat," I say. "I think the idea is that words don't matter. You sing like the music plays. It's easy. Sing easy. Speak easy. Like a universal language, you know?"

"That's infantile," he says. "The universal language is love. Obviously."

Sergei inserts a cassette in the deck, and now the car is filled with my past. It's one of the old love songs: "*Tyomnaya Noch*," "Dark Night." A soldier on the battlefield singing to his beloved far away. I remember how much Sveta loved this song. How she would dance all by herself to this song, no need for a partner.

I turn and gaze out the window at the fluorescent guardrails racing past, and beyond, the dark barges on the darker river. Both moving so much more slowly than this fast car, but still alongside us, parallel. I'm overwhelmed with loneliness.

Tyomnaya noch. Bullets whistling in the dark night . . . My love for you. Safe in the dark night.

It's strange. How a song that you've heard hundreds of times can, in the course of one night, suddenly reveal its meaning. *It is about you.* I'm listening to lyrics that

I know by heart, but they are an epiphany in this post-massacre mood I'm in: one part lovesick, one part lonesome. It's something I can imagine admitting to Ben, in one of our late-night telephone talks about music. I can imagine saying to him, "Every song is about you, when you're a little bit in love."

Am I in love? I wonder. *With whom?*

We've pulled off the highway and are stopped at a red light on the corner of Brighton Beach Avenue. The song is ending, the soldier praying that it's true that nothing will happen in the dark night, as long as he believes in his love.

Sergei puts one hand on his heart and proclaims, "Oy. Now that's music. A true Russki Romance."

I lean over and kiss him. Right there. On his lips, at the red light, as the song ends. But there is no fire. Just like the song promised. Though the soldier meant nothing bad would happen. For me, it's just . . . nothing.

The light turns green.

"Where's your house?" Sergei asks, his face still inches from mine.

I sit back in my seat and direct him down Brighton Beach Avenue. At the corner of Coney Island Avenue, Gosha crosses the glare of the headlights. I lean forward and watch him enter Corsair, Vova Skilarsky's joint. Brighton's own speakeasy. I wonder if Pop is inside, too, or if he's home, waiting for my report.

"Somebody you know?" asks Sergei, watching me watching Gosha.

I sit back again, casual. "You can let me out here. It's just up the street."

Sergei pulls to the curb and turns off the car. I'm struggling to open the door, desperate to get out, but he leans across me and plucks my hand from the handle.

"Marina. You are a very beautiful young lady and . . ." He chews his lip. For once, he is not in fully control. "It gives me great pleasure to be with you. To dance with you. But you've had a confusing night. Let me walk you home."

"No." I protest. "I'd prefer you didn't."

"Don't be like that. Do you think I don't want to . . ."

I won't look at him.

He pulls my hand to his lips and kisses it. "I just don't want to make this harder," he says.

"Sure." I say, though I have no idea what "this" is that he doesn't want to make "harder." I repress the urge to say something sarcastic and highly inappropriate. I just want to be alone. To be lonely. To skulk away, crawl into bed and listen to "Dark Night" over and over and over. I sigh. "I'm going to go."

"I'm walking you home," he insists. "I am."

I let him. We walk the three blocks to my building in silence. At the entry I thank him, but he's not having it. He wants to see me all the way up. I shrug, trying not to panic. I don't want Sergei to meet my father. I don't want my father to meet Sergei. I wish, at this moment, that I had never met him. Never danced with him. Never kissed him.

By the time we've climbed the three flights of stairs, Pop is in the landing.

"I thought that might be you," he says, half running down the stairs to meet us. He offers Sergei a hand. "Viktor. *Ochen rad.*"

"Sergei. Pleased to meet you."

"Come up. Come in. I just put on the kettle. Just for a minute."

Dear God. As if the night weren't already enough of a disaster. Falling in love, out of love, unconscious, self-conscious, too-conscious. As if I weren't already regretting every move I have made with Sergei, I am now watching my father make all the same mistakes.

"Pop, please," I hiss when we are inside. "It's not what you think."

But it's no use. Pop starts talking, hell-bent on making some sort of connection. We're scarcely in the door, and already he is parsing every detail of our life in America for Sergei's benefit. One moment cryptic, the next bizarre, he's a parody of a spook. I can't even keep up with his strange veiled references to know whether I need to confirm or cover them back up. But if my father's shambolic performance isn't strange enough, now Sergei seems to be playing along: picking up the hints, tossing them back just as casually.

"Yes. The Bolshoi has fallen on hard times. Dukovskaya, Danilov. I understand the US trip is in jeopardy. I'm sure I'm not alone in hoping that Svetlana Dukovskaya has not retired definitively." He pauses, stirring another spoonful of sugar into his tea. "It would be tragic to have lost so fine a dancer to obscurity."

Pop offers Sergei a cigarette. "A pointless loss. Nobody wins."

Sergei takes the cigarette, but rebuffs Pop's match. He taps it lightly on the table, distracted, it would seem, by thoughts of the regrettable fate of Svetlana Dukovskaya.

"These things, in my experience, are often political in nature. And, though I confess it's been years since I was anywhere close to the intrigue of Soviet Ballet, these things are sometimes . . . reversible."

There is eye contact. It's broken by footsteps in the hallway behind us. Dyadya Gosha steps into the room. I have a full fifteen seconds to gauge the faces of the three men now tasting the taboo taunt of Svetlana Dukovskaya in the air. Gosha is the first to speak.

"Double-booked, Vitya?"

"Georgi, have a seat. This young man is Marina's date. A fellow dancer at her new school. And a gentleman, I'm inclined to believe. Sit down, take some notes in civility."

But Gosha doesn't sit. He turns to me instead and says. "What's on your dress, Marya? Don't let me hear that you let you let your date mess your skirt."

"Dyad Gosh! *Stidno?*" I gasp. "I spilled, okay?"

"So go change."

They are all looking at me. Even Sergei, his grey eyes cold. I want to flee, but the hallway is only so long.

"Sergei, I think you should go now," I say. "Thank you for bringing me home."

He rises. Taps the virgin cigarette once more on the table. Then he clears his throat and says, "Marina had a bit of an episode tonight. Just dizziness. Nothing too serious. It's always hard for a young woman, a dancer especially, to keep in health. But added stresses . . . well.

I'm just glad I was there. To be of assistance. I'll keep an eye on her, I assure you." Sergei winks at me. But I can see through it. It is a well-practiced wink, I understand, harmless. "We're partners after all. *Da*, Marina?"

Pop is on his feet, pumping Sergei's hand. "Excellent. That's excellent. Sergei, a great pleasure to meet you. We will, I'm sure, meet again. Marina has done well to introduce us, no?"

Sergei holds the cigarette aloft. "I'll take this with me, then," he says. He slips into English. "A souvenir?"

He crosses over to me, kisses me on the cheek, steps around Georgi, and leaves.

Now it's just the three of us. Again, Gosha is the first to speak.

"You have blackouts now, too, eh, Marya? Vitya. You need to get this girl to a doctor. God knows, this is where it all went bad for Sveta. Started as blackouts."

"I don't need a doctor. He does," I snap, glaring at my father. "What are you, crazy? You think that stupid puppy had any idea what you were on about?"

"What were you on about, Vitya?" asks Gosha. The sparkle has gone out of his eyes. "What did you tell him?"

My father is struggling to light another cigarette. "Don't be blind," he hisses. "That boy's KGB. You heard him. 'We're partners, Marina and I.'"

"Pop. You're hearing what you want to hear."

Even as I say it I wonder what it is I want to hear. That Sergei was making small talk? That the way he has treated me is . . . what? Respectful? Chivalrous?

I wonder what I would think of Pop's theory if Sergei

had kissed me back. Or if he had been even a little bit startled by Pop's behavior. But he didn't and he wasn't. Does that mean that he has had other motivations all along? I had promised Pop I would look out for them— the spies in the ballet. And then I didn't even recognize him? Am I that giddy? That stupid? Or is my father that desperate?

I'm tired. Too tired to make sense. Too confused to make a sensible argument. But my father, after weeks of winding himself tighter and tighter in a story of intrigue, has finally sprung.

"Open your eyes," he pleads. "Sveta just whet their appetite. They want more. They want more and they are coming to find me to get more. But I've got it. You see? I've got it."

Pop holds his battered briefcase aloft. He tosses it on the table, unlocks the clasp and extracts a rectangular piece of plastic the size of his splayed hand. It's thin as a sheet of paper. A computer disc. A harmless floppy disc, yet full of God-only-knows what sort of harm. He fans the air with it. I know it can do nothing to us. Not in here. It needs a computer, a coat pocket, a hidden compartment. It needs to be handed from one spy to another in a complicated dance and then . . . what?

The memory of the papers in Gosha's bag flash before me. And my own sarcasm that night: *Why not call the CIA and offer to sell them germ weaponry in exchange for Sveta. Gospodi*, was this my idea?

"Don't be a fool, Vitya," says Gosha.

"*Durak?*" repeats my father. "*Kto zdes' durak*, Gosha?

Who's the fool? You couldn't get your hands on this kind of information if it was written on a hooker's ass."

"But only a fool would throw it away like you are about to do."

There is a long pause. Gosha reaches over and takes the floppy disc from Pop's hand. His voice is gentle when he speaks again.

"This is gold, Vitya. It's your future. You can do anything with this." He looks at me, at my disheveled dress and disbelieving eyes. "You can give Marya everything Sveta wanted for her."

I am going to be sick. It's not an episode; it's not gin; it's not regret or remorse or confusion. It's the look in these two men's eyes as they regard each other. I turn and run down the hall. In the bathroom I slam the door. My retching drowns out their voices in the front room. But when I emerge, exhausted and weak, I hear one last retort:

"Over my dead body."

I don't know whose voice it is.

ELEVEN
LIVE DANCING

The phone rings forever, but I don't answer it. Ten minutes later it rings again. I pull myself out of bed, step into my slippers, and head down the hall. Pop's bed is already put away. I wonder if he slept in it last night. I imagine him snoring on a dirty couch in the back room of the Corsair. I hope that some dancing girl brought him a blanket before he passed out.

"It's me," says Ben when I finally pick up.

"Hello, you."

"You okay?"

"Hmm."

"Okay. I just wanted to make sure. I . . . I shouldn't have let you go alone last night. I mean alone with him. I should have come. We should have come."

"I don't really blame you. I said . . . things."

He doesn't reply. A train pulls into the station across

the street. I watch a woman struggle to get her baby carriage onto the subway, three small children tugging at her skirts. We both speak at once.

"You were right." "I'm sorry." "Can I meet you somewhere?"

We agree on the boardwalk. In an hour.

I take a hot shower and dress, wondering what I will say to Benjamin Frame now that I have belittled him, seen his ugly side, made a fool of myself. And also confirmed that my father is playing with fire.

I don't go straight to the boardwalk. Instead, I walk up Brighton Beach Avenue, peering into every café. I want a cup of tea, but I also want Gosha. I want to hear his voice, gentle and sane. I want assurances that my father is just over-excited and exhausted. But that Gosha will bring him back to reality. Whatever that is.

I finally find him in Alyona's, alone at a table in the corner. He smiles when he sees me, and for a moment I can fool myself: None of it happened. It's just Dyadya Gosha. He's drinking tea, wearing spectacles, reading the paper. I can imagine a Sunday morning in Moscow, the smell of fried eggs in the kitchen, walking in to find Dyad Gosh. "Shhh," he would say. "Let's gobble them all up before your folks wake up."

I sit next to him. Alyona brings another teapot.

"What happened last night, Gosha?"

"I could ask you the same thing. What were you thinking, bringing that squig home. You know your father's got delusions."

"Are they, Gosha? Delusions? It was Sergei who first

mentioned Sveta. And about Lukino? He didn't bat an eye when Pop started in on the Geneva Conventions and lack of evidence and all that."

I pour the tea. Gosha is silent. He takes a sip. "You should eat something," he says. He tells Alyona to bring some kasha and sausage for me.

"And what about the *bratva*?" I ask. "I know Pop's got something going. What is it?"

He takes off his glasses, folds the paper and leans forward on his elbows, his head close to mine.

"It's all he has right now, Marya. I'm helping him develop, let's say, assets. These are valuable assets. And what I can do? I can find the best value for them. That means going through channels that are best greased. Channels that know all types of business. Deliver all types of assets. Arrange all sorts of delivery."

He falls silent when Alyona returns with the plate. The food before me couldn't look less appetizing, but Gosha nudges it closer.

"*Esh, dochka.* Eat."

I take a bite. I nearly gag.

"I don't think you know what you're doing," I say. "Either of you."

"It is complicated, yes. But it is also simple. Stupidly simple. But see, Vitya needs to be convinced. He needs to understand that . . ."

He pauses.

"Understand what?"

"That we can win a great deal. A very great deal. But perhaps not everything. Perhaps not Sveta. Not if he insists on believing that the KGB is holding her for ransom. Not if he thinks he can buy her back."

Gosha watches me closely. I don't know what he sees because I don't know what I show. I don't know how to react.

"Marya, your mother is sick. She was sick when she left you. And you know—you *know* that after what they have done to her, she is sicker now."

He reaches into the inside jacket of his pocket and coaxes a corner of the floppy disc into view. He jerks his chin at it.

"The information on this will not make her well. But it can kill. It can kill millions. I'm talking about a weapon: plague as aggression. Death to the US through the water supply. If your father lets it get into the hands of the KGB, that is what will happen. Sveta will be lost and no one will be safe. That's why I took it."

He closes his jacket over the disc. Casually, he leans over and cuts a piece of sausage, which he pops into his mouth. When he's done chewing he says, "From now on, Marya, you are the love of your father's life. Can you be that? If you can be that for him, I can help you both. But he must forget about saving Sveta. Sveta is lost."

I'm up so quickly I nearly upend the table. There is tea on the floor. The half-eaten sausage rolls off the plate, but I am already on the avenue running. I have to stop when I get to the boardwalk to bend over and sob. I'm remembering the vision of Sveta all alone behind a desolate barrier. A sick old lady. I'm still weeping when

I start running again. There's a figure ahead. I run faster, and I don't stop until I am in Ben's arms.

"SO YOU'RE TELLING ME that your mother is in a psychiatric ward; your father is making a deal with the KGB to get her out; your Dyadya is in possession of top-secret biochemical research. Oh, and Sergei is not just a douche; he's a Soviet agent."

I look at Ben. He's listening but I can see that he doesn't believe me. I don't care, because he still has both arms around me, and I can still feel his lips on the top of my head where he pressed them while I cried, whispering into my hair that it will all be okay, it will all be okay. I don't believe him, either. But this mutual skepticism feels intimate in a way that is closer than agreement.

"*Da, tochno.* It's crazy. But you were the one to warn me, right? About Pop's sniffing around. I don't know how he did it, but he has something that's worth something."

"But we don't know that," Ben murmurs.

"Not without a computer to see what's on that disc. Even then, I wouldn't know. I mean, how would I know the difference? Top-secret weapons, or somebody's research paper from nineteen seventy-two on fungus spores? I wouldn't know the difference."

"My father would," says Ben. He pushes a strand of hair from my face. His eyes are serious.

"Can you get the disc?" he asks.

I sigh and bury my head into his shoulder. I don't know how to do that. I can make Gosha trust me, but I don't think I can take from him something that he has already decided is "gold."

"This can't be happening," I say.

"But it *is* happening. Maybe you should stay out of it. Both of us. Maybe it's serious, Marya. Even if it isn't true. What do you want to do, wait for it to blow over? Blow up?"

"No," I say. I want to be strong. I want to be reasonable and brave and to show Ben that I can handle this. But I'm too emotional to be brave. I admit it.

"I just want my mother. I'd give them Pop. I swear it. He's the one should be in the *durdom*. She should be here with me."

I'm crying again, but Ben just holds me tighter. There's no more whispering. Maybe he knows everything's not going to be okay after all.

"I'm breaking up with Lindsay," he says after some time. I start to ask, but he cuts me off. "Don't worry. It was very amicable last night. I apologized, tried to make it up to her. I was a real gentleman once you left, honest. I bought her flowers, walked across the bridge with her. But I'm going to tell her that I can only be her friend. That's all."

"Why?" I ask.

He lifts my chin so that I'm looking in his eyes. I know why.

The moment passes too quickly. His gaze shifts to something over my shoulder. I turn and see my father staggering toward us up the boardwalk. He's bareheaded despite the wind, and a flash of skin reveals he's not wearing socks. My heart wants to break. My father truly is unwell. I want to jump up and run to him, wrap him in my arms. And I also want him to disappear. He stops midway, turns around and looks back down the boardwalk—back toward the lonely red Parachute Jump standing sentry over the shoreline. A metal souvenir of a time long ago, when people flocked to this beach for fun and sun, not just refuge. He stands still for a long time. When he turns back toward us, he's patting his coat pockets like he's lost something. He's looking at me without recognition. It wasn't me that he lost.

"Pop?"

He focuses and hurries over.

"Have you seen Gosha?" he asks, with a quick nod to Ben.

I consider the question.

"He was at Alyona's fifteen minutes ago. Why?"

Pop shifts on his feet. "What are you doing here?" he asks with another glance at Ben.

"Talking," I say.

Ben speaks up. "Marina thinks that perhaps you have some material that you would like my father to take a look at, Mr. Ivanov. Some work that is not yet peer reviewed?"

I look at him, wide-eyed. This was not something we had planned.

"I'd be happy to take it to him, if that would be all right with you," Ben continues, his gaze steely.

I don't know what Ben expected my father to say to this. Did he think he would be grateful for the offer? Pull out a ream of stolen papers and say, "Thanks, sonny, let me know what he thinks?"

"It's too late for that," says my father. "It's too late."

"What do you mean?" I ask. He doesn't answer. I extricate myself from Ben and pull my father to the side. "Pop, what do you mean? What is going on? What happened last night? Have you been out all night?"

He turns his back and says softly into the wind, "Can you find Sergei? You have to get him to come soon. I faked him out, Gosha. It's a fake. But once he gives it to them, I don't know if . . ."

"Who's 'them'? Who's he going to give it to, Pop?"

"Just get home and wait for Sergei to call. He'll call. Sure he will. We need him to come back soon. I can't talk now, *dochka*. Get home. And keep that one out of it," he says jerking his head at Ben. "You have to be on my side. You promised. We're not done yet."

With that, he bolts for the street. "Pop," I call. But he's gone, deaf to me.

I walk back to Ben, shivering in the wind. "He's delusional. He's off his rocker."

Ben is watching my father disappear. "I'm reading a biography about Shostakovich. You know what he said? Right around the time he was being hounded by Stalin during the purges? When he was in the middle of his Fifth Symphony and was sleeping in the hallway so that his family wouldn't be woken if he was arrested in the night?"

I shake my head.

"He said, 'When a man is in despair, it means he still believes in something.'"

• • •

I SPEND ALL AFTERNOON at home with Pop, armed with five different videotapes from the movie store downstairs. We watch all our old favorites and eat blini with jam. From time to time, Pop lifts the receiver on the phone to check for a dial tone. Each time I surreptitiously replace the wad of paper that keeps it disconnected. Keeps the world out of our house. No Gosha. No Sergei. No Lindsay. I stay close. Rub his shoulders. Laugh too loud at the funny parts. I only go out once, to buy him cigarettes and to call Ben from a pay phone.

"I'm just trying to keep him calm. Almost, like sedated."

"Probably a good idea. So what are you going to do?" he asks. "What are *we* going to do?"

"I don't know. I think I'm going to go watch *Happy-Go-Lucky*. Then maybe I'll decide."

"Okay. Keep me posted, all right? I'm . . ." Ben pauses and then slips into English. "I've got your back."

I don't know the expression. I think of Sergei's hand on my back. I reject it. I only want Ben's.

SOMEHOW I MAKE IT to Monday, feeling much less cavalier and no more certain. When I wake up I know that I still can't face an afternoon of dance. I call Juilliard and plead sick. And I lie to Pop. I tell him that Sergei said he would come by at some point during the day. It's the only way I can be sure he will stay home and not go do something bizarre. But I have to get out of that apartment. School is suddenly an oasis. Plus, there's someone I want to see.

At lunch Lindsay plops down next to me, in high spirits.

"Hey, you! Your phone is on the fritz. What do you hear from that sexy swing dancer? That boy is sooo fine."

"Yeah, well, he's good dancer," I answer, my eyes on my tray.

"Um. Understatement of the year. Ohmygosh Marya, can I have him when you are done with him, huh?"

I laugh, suddenly thinking of that girl who had said the same about my *dublonka*. It seems like a lifetime ago. What was her name, that pug-nosed girl who so envied my coat?

"I think maybe he's done already with me. I kissed him. But he acted like I just asked his face 'Hey, what time it is?'"

"Huh. That's kinda tight." Lindsay furrows her brow. "Maybe he thought you were having a weird seizure or something. So what was that, anyway? Ben says you had some sort of a spell?"

"What did you guys do on Saturday, after?" I ask, changing the subject and not just to change the subject. I want to know about the flowers, the bridge. *I'm going to break up with Lindsay.* I want to know about that.

"Oh. Just had a heart-to-heart and walked half the damn way home," she says. "You would have been very impressed with me. You ever tried to walk across the Brooklyn Bridge in high heels? And in thirty degree temperature?"

"I only understand Celsius."

"Well, it was cold. And you were gone—in a warm car with a super fine gentleman, and I was with Ben, grouch overlord, walking home. You know what I mean?"

"Not really?" I ask. I don't understand why she is so, what's the word? *Chipper.*

"Ben. A grouch. Totally. Such an asshole. So, on the other side of the bridge I told him, 'Ben. You don't deserve me. I'm going to date other men. Now hail a cab for me.'" She laughs. "So you let that Sergei know that I'm available."

I want to laugh and cry all at once. "Okay," I say stupidly.

"And for the record . . . so is Ben."

She doesn't look at me when she says this. I wait a second before answering. "I don't think Sergei is interested in Ben. But I'll let him know."

That makes her laugh. "God love ya, Marya. You're the best."

"I'm not going to Juilliard today," I tell her. "Maybe we can go get tea after school, just for little while. Then I have to get home. Pop is . . . sick."

Lindsay squirms. "Well, actually. I mean—I know I said I broke up with him, but actually, um, Ben asked if he could pick me up after school."

"Oh," I say. I'm confused.

"I wasn't making it up, Marya. Well, I mean a little bit, about how I told him off like that. But honest. It's over. I'm no fool. Ben wouldn't miss class if it weren't something important. He'll just, you know, confirm it."

Now I get it. I see the future. Sveta saw the past. But

only Lindsay is clear-eyed enough to see what's going on right now. I reach across her enormous backpack and hug her. I can see she is genuinely concerned that I thought she had lied. And me with the secrets I'm keeping. *Stidno.* I'm ashamed.

The bell rings. It's two o'clock, and I'm free to go. All I can think is that, in a matter of hours, Ben will be, too.

WALKING HOME I'M SO deep in my head it takes me a moment to realize I'm being tailed. There's a car just behind me, purring along at a snail's pace. I turn. A familiar sports-car. Sergei is back.

He leans over to the passenger door and opens it.

"Get inside." His voice is clipped.

Uh-unh. Hell, no.

"Did you just talk to my father?" I ask.

"No. I was looking for you."

"Why?"

"They told me you were sick. I was worried."

"*Chush sobachi,*" I mutter. "Bullshit."

I glance down the street. I can see the neon sign of Corsair. Two girls in cheap furs are knocking at the door. Live Dancers, just as the sign promises. Must be opening time. Sure enough, loud, recorded, electronic music spills out. Nothing live about it. Two thirty in the afternoon can be any hour of day or night under the disco lights and pallor of a place like Corsair.

It also occurs to me that at any moment my father or Gosha could walk in or out of those doors. I don't want Sergei to see that. So I get in.

"Drive," I say.

He pulls away from the curb. His tires squeal lightly.

"Why did you come all the way down here?" I ask. "It wasn't to play truant officer."

"You're right," he says. "I'll be straight with you. Up until Saturday night my only objective was to get to know you. Get you to trust me. Get you to tell me who you are. Confirm who you are, I should say. I'm interested in your parents. I don't want you getting hurt. But now we know that the lay of the land is different. We have many objectives now. Your safety is still one of them."

It takes my breath away, but I'm not that surprised. In a way, I am relieved. Pop is a mess, but he isn't as crazy as I'd suspected. We're headed down Surf Avenue toward Coney Island. The road is flanked on one side by high-rise apartment buildings that seem to be plucked from the outskirts of any city in the Communist Bloc. On the other side are the desolate grounds of an off-season amusement park. I feel trapped between the familiar and the foreign.

Sergei pulls a U-turn and parks the car directly in front of an enormous and derelict roller coaster.

"All right. Tell me," I say, fighting to keep my voice steady. "Who are you, really?"

"The more important question is, who are you? Your mother is Svetlana Dukovskaya. Where is she now?"

"Institutionalized," I say. "I don't know where."

"You're saying she is in the Soviet Union. She didn't get out?"

"No." I glare at him. That handsome face, a face that turned me to gelatin, now looks lost. "Wait, I don't know—maybe. What do you know?"

"What about Danilov?"

"Who, Arkady Grigorievich? What about him?"

"He's been absent from the Bolshoi since January."

"What? He defected?"

No answer.

"Is my mother with him?"

Silence. The windshield is beginning to fog over.

"Levshik. Georgi," he prompts. "What about him?"

"What about him?" I ask. "I wish I knew. He says my mother is alive. He saw her on New Year's Day. And then he fled."

"How did you get out?" he asks now.

"On a plane. On a goddamn plane." I switch to English. "Tattoo you! What *do* you know?"

A sad smile flits over his lips. "How much does your father know about Lukino?"

"I don't know," I answer truthfully.

Sergei is silent, stroking the steering wheel with his leather gloves. "You cold?" he asks now, making a motion to turn on the heater. I shake my head. The idea of his hands anywhere near the cassette deck makes me sick to my stomach.

"Is my father in danger?" I ask.

"He is. You are. We all are." He turns to me, his eyes on mine. I can't believe that I could have ever thought they were the eyes of a flirt.

"We believe that your father may have some highly

sensitive information. In the wrong hands . . . it could be a threat to national security. I need your assistance. I need you to secure it. I had hoped to be able to safeguard it with the help of your mother. But I can see now that it's not your mother controlling the situation."

I'm trying to sort this out. Sergei wants the floppy disc. Pop wants to give it to him. So where is the disconnect? Why is Sergei so hung up on Sveta, and where she is? Something's wrong.

"What about my mother?" I ask.

Sergei rubs a spot on the fogged-in windshield. Once more, we can see the grey skeleton of the roller coaster. The faded sign that reads RIDE AGAIN, $1.

"Our people are working on it. Trying to expedite an exchange. The Embassy is making arrangements, but without Danilov . . ."

"What exactly does Danilov have to do with this?" I ask.

"He has been pulled from the US tour. He won't be coming to New York next week. We have to act now."

I roll this over in my head. *The Embassy. Our people. National security.* His perfect English, his deliberate dismissal of jazz. It dawns on me. Sergei works for the Americans. He can no more release Sveta than he can liberate Lukino of its illicit stockpiles and secrets. He's not KGB. He's CIA. My father bet wrong. And Gosha . . .

"I'll see what I can do," I say. I have to get home. Immediately.

"I'll drive you back," he says, his fingers on the ignition.

"No. No way. Let me out of the car." This time I'm firm.

He pulls a small card and a pen from his inside pocket. Scribbles on it and hands it to me.

"I need to hear from you in the next twenty-four hours, or I will have to proceed."

I glance at the card. It's not embossed. It's not fancy. It's a card with a Russian boy's handwriting spelling a Russian boy's name. But I believe it. This Russian boy is working for the American government. He is a spy. He is a traitor.

"How did you get into this?" I ask. I raise my eyes, suddenly more curious than cautious. "And why? You're a beautiful dancer—isn't that enough?"

"I know," he says softly. "And it would be. Enough. Except that now I am part of this. It doesn't matter why, Marya. You and I are both part of it. Work with me and we can both get out safely. Everyone can."

I get out of the car without another word.

There is rain blowing with me all the way up Surf Avenue. I can't see it, even from this close, but the ocean sounds rough. My ears are full of its misplaced roar. And something else. An unwanted melody about bullets in the night air and wind in the wires.

By the time I reach Brighton Beach, I am soaked through. My feet squelch in their boots and my hair sticks to the back of my neck. I see a haze of red lights up ahead. A cloud of brakes, vehicles, police cars, and an ambulance. In front of Corsair, a police cordon of yellow tape.

Tyomnaya Noch. I feel the darkness fall, but it's not yet night.

I ignore the shouts, duck under the tape, push through the doors. A clutch of near-naked women, live dancers, pushes back, corralled by a police officer. Directed by some unknown power, I forge ahead into this shadowy den, its live dancing music now dead, killed by the cops. Another officer steps in front of the door before me, and I nearly knock him down. I skid to a halt in a small back room lit by a single overhead bulb. A sagging couch, a calendar from 1980, a poster of Bo Derek, a plaque from the Veterans of the Afghan War with the name Vladimir Skilarsky on it . . . a metal door behind a bare desk, open to the alleyway where more cops mill about.

I take all this in and more: In front of the desk, face down in a bloody puddle, lies my father. Next to him is Gosha on his back, also covered in blood.

"Get her outta here!" hollers a cop, pointing a finger at me.

The EMT people bustle in and push me aside to lift Gosha onto a stretcher. But before they do, Gosha opens his eyes and says, very clearly:

"I ain't sayin' nothing."

PART FOUR

BRIGHTON BEACH FEBRUARY 1983

MUSIC
TO LIVE BY

TWELVE
PATHETIQUE

It is several hours before a man with no uniform enters the interrogation room and tells me what I already know: My father has been murdered. He shows me a badge in his wallet, then tells me that my father's death was the culmination of an altercation with one (he checks his notes) Georgi Levshik in the back room of the Corsair nightclub. The cause of the dispute was likely mob-related, which is why he is here. This man with the concealed badge represents some sort of anagram— I don't really register which one. PDA? BFD? FDA? TGIF? Whatever it is, it's not the CIA.

"Are you CIA?" I ask once more.

"No. But there will be cross-agency cooperation. A formality, given your father's recent arrival and status as a Soviet citizen."

Parsing the man's careful speech is a strange exercise. Do I know more or less than him? Is he trying to give or to get information? Why is the CIA a "formality?" Does he know about Sergei? Does he want to solve a murder or frame a mobster? Or does he just want to check the box that is "inform family members and provide for dependencies," and go home to his own wife and kids?

My body aches as if I have been beaten, though no one has touched me. Not since they dragged me from the Corsair and drove me four blocks to the precinct house. Someone did bring me coffee—a woman. She even sat next to me in silence while I stared numbly at the gallery of Most Wanted. It had seemed so American, the corkboard full of malevolent men with their police-sketch scars and crosshatched broken noses. But then I realized that the only ones with identities, with names printed below their dangerous caricatures, were the Russians.

"Georgi Levshik is my father's friend," I say. "His only friend here."

I am not protesting Gosha's role as the prime suspect; in my heart I know that Gosha is capable of terrible destruction, just as he is capable of deep devotion. And I'm not trying to infuse this case with sentiment. Why should I make this WTF man understand that there is a story that starts somewhere beyond Brighton Beach, sometime before the last straw was not enough to hang onto? I am only stating a fact—Georgi Levshik is my father's best friend—so that I can ask an important question: "Will he survive?"

"Who? Levshik? It looks like he dodged the bullet tonight—actually two. The third one got him, though.

It lodged in his ribcage. Some internal bleeding. He's in intensive care but stabilized. And he won't talk."

"How do you know he shot my father?"

"It was his gun. Witnesses put them in the back room alone. There was audible disagreement. Right now we're just trying to figure out who fired first, Levshik or your father."

Audible disagreement. This man speaks fluent euphemism. Pop and Gosha had a fucking brawl. And no one was there to intercede. For a moment I feel that it is my fault. I nurse the idea long enough to feel tears sting my eyes. I haven't cried yet and I want to. I tell myself again: *This is my fault.* It's like looking up at the sun to coax a sneeze. But the crying doesn't come.

I run my fingers over the small card in my pocket. Sergei's number. Why hasn't he shown up? Just three hours ago he had set the clock and given me a deadline. Yet here we are: Pop dead. Gosha hospitalized. The disc a question mark; and he's nowhere?

American expressions rattle through my head: *All bets off. Tables turned.* If there is to be "cross-agency cooperation," then where is the CIA? Are they that slow and sloppy, or is Sergei a liar? Because the only explanation for this sudden disappearance is personal involvement. He wanted the disc. How far would he go to get it? As far as the Corsair?

I should tell this man.

No way will I tell this man.

Better that he should tell me.

"So you are sure they were alone back there?" I ask.

He leans back in the chair and looks me over. I see his demeanor change. I'm no longer the dead man's daughter, in need of an explanation and probably a place to stay. I'm a piece of the puzzle.

"Let me ask you this. Is there someone who you would expect to join your father and Levshik in the back room of the Corsair?"

I shrug. "It is Vova Skilarsky's club."

"He has an alibi. A tight one."

"He has guys. There is one guy. Handsome guy with gabardine coat and leather gloves," I say.

"You want to give me a name?" he asks.

No. No, I don't. I don't want to give anything to anyone.

"What about . . ." I can't remember the English. What about *dokazatel'stva*? Things left at the scene of a crime? Things like floppy discs. I pass my hand over my forehead and say something about being mixed up and can I have a glass of water. When he comes back I tell him I need to make a phone call.

"Of course," he says, rising. "My understanding is that you have no other relatives in this country? The FBI will be assigning a case officer—"

"No." I interrupt. "I don't need. Just let me make telephone call. You allow me to leave now, right? I'm not suspect and I'm not dependent. Not state dependent," I clarify, translating precisely from the Russian. We have all sorts of terminology for wards of the state—we are, after all, guaranteed beneficence "from cradle to grave."

It strikes me as intensely sad, that thought. My father, just a month out of the Motherland, has been robbed of the only comfort a Sovog can count on. *Your grave will be far from home, Pop.*

The man brings a phone into the room and waits.

"I can have privacy," I tell him, with a silent thanks to my civics teacher.

He steps out and leans against the door. The phone cord is stretched taut beneath it. I can see the back of his head through the small window above the doorknob. The nape of his neck is angry and red. Someone shaved him too close.

I pull the card from my pocket. It has two numbers on it. One is Manhattan. One Brooklyn. I think back to the moment in Sergei's car when I realized that he would take what he could get without giving anything in return. That Pop and Gosha both had it wrong. That the KGB was not following us, not monitoring us, not preparing to slide my mother's trauma into a brief-case to be swapped in the fog of the boardwalk. That's when I knew we had walked unmolested out of Russia's clutches and straight into the hands of a whole new crew of jealous bastards. I don't know if Sergei believed me. If he trusts me. Did he follow me? Did he find out? That the secrets of Lukino were being haggled over in the headquarters of the *bratva* boss? Could he have taken matters into his own hands? Could he have put a gun into someone else's hands?

I realize that I have folded the card into thirds. It is an accordion of options: ally, enemy, killer. I can make

Sergei any of these. All I know is that he is no longer my dance partner.

I take a deep breath and dial.

"Hello?"

"Hello. It's Marya. I need to speak to Ben, Mrs. Frame."

HOW MANY MORNINGS IN the past three months have I woken up dead? Dead because the life I knew when I went to sleep was gone at dawn. Five mornings in a row I awoke dead in Moscow, dead to the changes wrought in my Krasnopresnya apartment. At least as many mornings, random and heavy, I watched the Atlantic ebb from a new window, only joining the living when I physically collided with a body on the boardwalk or Brighton Beach Avenue.

Cross the oceans, but do not cross me . . .

Prostite, I would apologize.

I repeated it last night. Over and over. *Prostite menya*—forgive me.

A stupid thing to say to Ben's parents, who took me in, horrified and bewildered, and plied me with tea and then tissues and then words bland and sweet and useless and well-meaning.

We sat in the kitchen, turning our cups in circles, waiting for the next thing to happen, waiting for an answer. When the news came on the radio, Dr. Frame quickly turned it off and hurried into the next room so that he could listen out of earshot. Afterward he had nothing to report, and I didn't ask. Mrs. Frame poured more tea and I apologized again, because there was nothing else to say.

Prostite menya. I'm sorry. Forgive me.

"Hush, child," she had said. "You have nothing to apologize for."

But I wasn't so sure. Because at midnight, Ben still was not home, and I could see worry flit across his parents' faces. In between slogans of sympathy and gestures of sincerity, they huddled together in the corner and wondered why their son had not called. I heard Dr. Frame on the phone with Lindsay's parents. Heard him say, "Isn't it awful" and "We'll just have to see" and "It's so unlike them." I heard them wondering if maybe they already know and are terribly upset. Of course they are. Must be terribly upset. It's so awful so horrible we'll just have to see.

I heard him assure whoever was on the other end of the phone, "She's with us. She'll be staying with us."

But I saw his eyes shoot sideways through the kitchen door. My presence for Ben's absence. Not a good exchange.

When Mrs. Frame insisted that I go to bed I didn't argue. I knew what it meant, falling asleep. It meant this day would end. This life, a short and sad excuse for the life I'd already lost, would be over. I would wake up, once more, dead.

And now it is morning and Mrs. Frame is sitting on the side of the bed, Ben's bed, stroking my shoulder.

I am awake but not alive.

"Did he come home?" I ask.

She shakes her head.

No, I am not even alive. My life is over. No Moscow, no mother, no father, no Ben.

"But there is another man here to see you. A young man. I asked him to come back later but he says it is important. It's about your father. His name is Sergei."

I'm awake now. I'm halfway downstairs when I hear Dr. Frame's angry voice from the kitchen. "We have every right to some answers since we're the only people that girl has . . ."

He falls silent when I enter. Sergei asks if we can have the room to ourselves. Dr. Frame looks ready to protest but his wife leads him out, the Western saloon-style door swinging shut behind them. Sergei takes a seat at the table and pulls a chair out for me. He is still in his coat. He looks as though he has not taken it off since I saw him yesterday. He looks as if he hasn't slept since then, either.

"Please accept my deepest condolences. I assure you, this is not how we anticipated it evolving."

I feel a sharp stab of pain. My father is no longer in danger. My father is dead.

"Condolences," I murmur. "Does that mean that you had nothing to do with this? Or does it mean that you botched something up but good and you hope I will forgive you?"

"Yesterday, after you left, I drove straight back to Lincoln Center," he says. "You can confirm it with anyone. I'm a dancer, Marina. That's the truth. I'm also an informant. But my authority goes only as far as information-gathering. Cultivation. I'm not an agent. I'm certainly not an assassin."

Cultivation. Sergei was cultivating me. To gather information for him. For him to gather for them. There is always somebody else to do your work for you. That never changes. I try to reconcile these two Sergeis. The one who, in the middle of rehearsal, learned that his mark had been whacked, and the one who sits before me with a ten o'clock shadow and a twitch in his left eye.

"I can only imagine what must be going on in your mind right now, Marina."

"I don't think that is true."

He looks out the window. A small bird, a winter bird, is tapping on the glass, curious.

"I wish I could give you time. I wish I could just stand aside and let you deal with this, your loss," he says quietly. "But I can't. The disc. It's still out there. The danger, I'm afraid, did not die with your father. I need you to get it back."

It seems a preposterous request. The kind of request that should come from a haggard colonel with an eye patch and two rows of medals across his chest. Or from a bearded revolutionary with nothing to lose. Or from a man with a gun at my back. But Sergei is none of those things.

"How can they have left this to you?" I ask. "Since when is preventing biological Armageddon the job for an 'informant'? What kind of spy organization recruits a seventeen-year-old girl and some Rostov Casanova to secure its super-secrets? *Gospodi*, my god! Do you really think I can just ask the mafia to please give me back that thing that my dad left in Vova's office?"

"Lower your voice," he says. His look is quick. "These people—the Frames, their son—they are, could be, implicated. Dr. Frame's name has been mentioned in more than one of your father's conversations. There is a good chance that the disc will be used against him. It could expose him. It could ruin him. It could send him back to the USSR. He doesn't deserve that, Marina, any more than you do. I want . . ." He glances at the doorway. "I want to prevent that."

"The Frames have no idea what my father was up to. Or why," I insist. "None. Keep them out of it or I swear I will blow this up. I will go to the police and tell them you were in the vicinity when it happened."

He looks at me, his eyes shot through with red. "Listen to me, Marya. I promise you I had nothing to do with your father's death. But I don't know about my higher-ups. And the FBI—let's just say they have their own loose cannons, too. And their own agenda. But I know that they want the disc. And they wanted your father alive."

"I wanted my father alive, too."

He flinches.

I hear the phone ring in the hallway. Ben's mother's voice high and anxious.

"The disc," says Sergei. "The *bratva* has it?"

I don't know. I don't know anything.

"Of course the *bratva* has it," I say. "Now go seduce

Vova Skilarsky's daughter and let me mourn my father in peace."

He stands and walks. At the kitchen door he turns back around.

"I am so very sorry," he says.

Prostite. Forgive me.

I watch his face slide, his features tremble in their perfect positions, his composure slip. I see Sergei struggle with something much stronger than uncertainty, much deeper than distrust. I feel a low vibration, a faint current left ungrounded by the short circuit that danced so briefly between us a short time ago. For one moment, I am sorry for him, because he is sorry for me. And then I turn my back on him and let him slip away, unforgiven.

CONEY ISLAND HOSPITAL IS a quick bus ride from the Frames's house. Mrs. Frame had insisted that I wait until her husband or the FBI man could accompany me, so I waited. Until she went to lie down with a migraine. Then I left a note on the counter and went alone

Now, my forehead rattling against the cold glass, I'm rehearsing what I will say when I see Georgi. I can't get further than "What happened in there?" How can I know what I will say after that? It's like knowing how loud you will scream when the forest divulges what lurks in its depth.

Up ahead, a crowd of tardy kids straggles into Bay High School. I wonder if Lindsay is among them. It had been her on the telephone earlier, but she told Ben's mother that she couldn't talk to me, she was late for school. Dina Frame relayed this to me in a strange voice, as though she didn't understand the words herself. "Of course, she is terribly upset, Marina. About your father. Some people don't process shock well, you know that. She asked me to give you a big hug. Americans, you know, put great stock in hugs, for some reason."

Mrs. Frame sighs. She hardly resembles the vivacious hostess I met New Year's Eve. She's worried and uncertain and she keeps her real thoughts to herself.

"What did she say about Ben?" I asked.

She raised her eyebrows high. I recognized it as a warning: *You're not going to like this one either.*

"She said that Ben has decided he needs a few days to himself. He is staying with friends in the city."

I watched Mrs. Frame suddenly become very intent on removing a smudge from her collar. I watched her worry the fabric, a deep crease down her forehead. I waited. Finally she looked me in the eye.

"She said that she would let him know what has happened. But that . . ." She frowned and her eyes could not hold mine. ". . . that it might take a few days."

I'm watching Bay High School slide past and wondering what could have made Ben desert me. Two days ago he'd promised me everything. Or did he?

Now that I think about it, I can't remember any concrete assurances, no confirmations. Except that he said he would be there for me. And the way he had said it made me think that he meant something more. Made me think that I would want him there for me. Would maybe

even, want there to be a reason why I would need him
to be there for me. I have a sick feeling, the same nausea
that I felt in the precinct house last night. Did I cause
this? Did I drive Ben away by bringing him too close?
Did I tell Ben that I am in love with him? Did I make him
think he was in love with me?

I must have misunderstood. Obviously I had gotten
Lindsay completely wrong. I thought she was making
room for me, as a gesture of friendship and understanding. I thought that she was making a supremely graceful
exit, but not that she was leaving *me*.

THE BUS TURNS ONTO Brighton Beach Avenue and we pass
Alyona's café, then the Corsair, and now, my building. Impulsively I pull the signal cord. I don't want to
see Gosha. I don't want to find out what happened. I
want to go home. But by the time the bus stops, I have
changed my mind again. There is no home. There is only
an empty apartment that has failed as a home. Failed as
shelter. So I sit back.

From across the street, the hospital is every bit as
large as our hospitals in Moscow. Inside, it is another
thing altogether. At home, you traverse vast foyers and
empty corridors just to get a pass that allows you access
to the sick. Otherwise, you're cut off. You wait with the
healthy, with books and with snacks and, often, with a
bottle. That great big edifice, and still you come ready to
subsidize the state's all-healing care.

But here, I have only just stepped inside the door and
already I am surrounded by nurses armed with gurneys

and clipboards; by families and their children clutching balloons and doll babies; by nuns and Koreans and
those pony-tailed Indians in robes, all distributing pam-
phlets and prayers. Elevators open and close on either
side, disgorging people who laugh and cry. I smell food
under red lights in the cafeteria to my right and the cloying scented candles in the flower shop to my left.

I am strangely relieved. This is just another public forum in America. Same but different. It's like I've
landed at a busy intersection. Coney Island Hospital just
shrugs its shoulders at my peculiar request: "I'm looking
for Georgi Levshik. Where do I find him?"

The answer is in a binder next to the computer.

He's been released from intensive care and is in monitoring. I take the elevator to the third floor and identify
Gosha's room from the policeman standing (not quite at
attention) outside the door. He looks me up and down
and then lets me in, saying, "Door stays open. I'll be
right outside."

Dyadya Gosha is propped up in the bed. His head
is turned away from me, toward a window covered by
a crooked plastic Venetian blind. I hesitate, but he has
heard me. Now he looks. His face is gaunt. His eyes are
alert. An IV dangles in his arm and his hospital gown
has slipped to expose a freckled shoulder.

"Marya, *dochka*, my poor darling. Come close."

I do. Here I am. I am right here. I'm at my uncle
Gosha's side and knowing that it has to be true. That
he is why my father is dead. Who else could have killed
Pop? Especially if the day after his murder, there is just

one policeman and a nurse with squeaky shoes outside
the hospital room of the prime suspect? Even in this
circus that is Coney Island Hospital, would a killer be
left unguarded if he had muscle behind him? The only
explanation for the normalness of this scene is that it
is normal. That it happens all the time. My father, an
American nobody, was shot and killed by his best friend,
a nobody in America. As soon as he stabilizes, he will
be arrested, tried, and jailed. And I still can't believe it.

"Did you do it?" I ask.

Gosha sighs and turns his face back to the window.

"You still don't trust me. You never trust me," he
says, his voice rough. "Maybe you were right. I mis-
calculated with your father, Marya. I never thought he
would do this. Put the gun to his own head."

"His own head," I repeat.

"Metaphorically." He faces me again. "*Nyet, dochka.*
I did not shoot Vitya. He shot me. You see? They pulled
a bullet from my chest last night. Hurts like hell, but
I will be fine in a few days. Vitya shot me, Marya. He
fucking went crazy, and he pulled out a gun and he shot
me. And when he did that . . . well, in short, he was
done."

He puts a finger against his temple, Russian roulette.

"I saw the body, Gosha. They were not self-inflicted
wounds. It was your gun that killed him." I hear the
emotion in my voice. I can feel it, too, and I wonder if
finally the dam will burst. "You two idiots went into
that mob den and started playing High Noon. What did
you say to him? Was it Ma? Was it that stupid disc?"

"No. It was bad luck," Gosha says quietly. "I have done bad things, it's true. I'm no angel, thanks God. But this time—I only wanted to do what was best. For you and for Vitya. You know I would never hurt you. None of you. Not your parents and not you. Never. You are my family." He chokes. They are real tears. "I love Vitya. But he shot me. He shot me."

"And who shot him?" I ask.

He is silent. It is a deliberate silence.

"If not you, who? I'm telling you, Gosha, if you are protecting some lowlife mobster, then you are even more pathetic than if you did this yourself."

"Pathetic," he murmurs. "*Pateticheskaya, pathetique.* It is a symphony, isn't it Marya? And a dark one at that." He shakes his head. "They brought me flowers, at least. The low-life mobsters." He nods to the far wall. I turn and see a vase full of lilies. Flowers for funerals. You never give lilies to a sick man. I guess it's something they picked up in America. Like a dead canary on the doorstep.

"Who did it?" I hiss. "Did your new friends show up, Gosha, is that what happened?"

"*Nyet dochka*, not my friends. Not *my* friends."

The nurse comes in with a tray of pills. "You should not be in here, young lady," she says.

"She was just leaving," replies Gosha. He reaches out and grasps my hand. I am surprised at how soft his skin is. His voice is tender. *Prosti menya, Marya.*

Yeah. I've heard that before.

• • •

I EXIT THE HOSPITAL and the sun smacks the outside world. I look right, north—toward the rest of Brooklyn, unknown—and beyond to the pinnacled skyline of Manhattan. In between here and there is a massive cemetery: a kilometer, if not more, of headstones gleaming white in the winter sun, nubbed teeth in a freakish flat skull.

Cemeteries. Funerals. Formalities of this tragic turn of events. In any other circumstance, Gosha would have been the person I'd entrust to figure this part out. How do I bury my father? How do I rise from the dead? But there are too many riddles to unravel before I can face the straight-up conundrums of capitalist death transactions.

I head south, back to my neighborhood. Back to the avenue and my empty apartment and my clueless high school and my suspicious benefactors. Why would anyone trust me? I can imagine Dina Frame, twisting her necklace around a manicured forefinger as her husband and the man with the FBI badge and Sergei himself all weave their web of conjecture around her. I imagine her screaming when I arrive at the door, like the survivors in that body snatcher movie Lindsay and I watched last Friday. I imagine her pointing, eyes on fire: I am a parasite, a plague, a contagion to be contained. I imagine her whispering over the phone to her son, "Stay away. Stay where you are until I tell you it's safe."

The sun is too bright. The breeze is too warm. The rain that soaked me yesterday is a dream. My life has fully collapsed on this, one of the most beautiful days I can remember since arriving.

In the medians of Ocean Parkway, the old people

have come out to warm up. They sit on the benches facing the sun, soaking something like life into their old bones. The friskiest have brought their backgammon boards and their political opinions. They spar in ancient languages. Again, a racking sadness. Why couldn't Pop have been granted this, America's second-place prize? No wealth, no fame, no fortune. But a February weekday under barren trees, the sun cutting stripes across old age. I pass an octogenarian couple. She wears a kerchief. He uses a cane. They have no need of conversation. But he holds her hand.

And at last, the tears come. A pathetic symphony.

By the time I reach the boardwalk I am drained and chilled, though the sun is still bright. The sea dances with whitecaps and acrobatic gulls. Is there no propriety in Brighton today? No respect for the dead?

I walk east on the boardwalk until I stand below my own window. My keys are in my pocket, and I grip them hard enough to leave their teeth in my palm.

In moments I am up the stairs, turning the key in the lock. I step into silence and the smell of mildew: a sink full of dishes, dishrags, and detritus. I close the door softly behind me.

There are stories in Russia of children whose parents disappear forever in the middle of the night. We all know that the fates of those children were grim. They were sent to the camps or to an orphanage or a rehabilitation center for the dependents of "enemies of the people." But the worst stories, the stories that haunted me most, were the stories of children who were allowed to reenter society. After their years of suffering were over, they were assigned residential quarters in a corner of the very same flat where their parents had been arrested a decade before. This is the story that fills me now with despair.

I don't know how long I have been sitting at the front door, shivering despite my sun-warmed jacket, when the phone jolts me from my stupor. I don't move, just let it drill a hole in my head until I hear my own voice ask the caller to leave a message.

There is a long silence and then a familiar voice.

"Marya. It's me. I know you are not there. I know you are safe. My parents will take care of you. But I wanted to hear your voice . . . God, Marya."

It's Ben. But not Ben. He sounds wrong, and he makes no sense. He has called because I'm not there. He is talking because he can't talk. He wants me to forgive him but he's done something unforgivable.

"Marya. I'm . . ."

I don't know why I can't move. Sunlight floods the kitchen and creeps toward me where I huddle by the door in my confusion. Ben is still speaking, but I only hear Gosha.

Nyet dochka—not my friends. Not my friends.

I rise, unsteady, and move toward the phone. I stumble over obstacles—desk drawers overturned, pillows ripped and disgorged, cassette tapes unspooled and disemboweled. I am almost to the phone—*not my friends*—and I hear Ben say, "*Prosti menya*. Forgive me."

I will suffocate from all these expressions of remorse.

The phone goes dead. But not before one other message is transmitted. It is in the background, just barely audible—an orchestral flourish and a lusty plea: "Don't Cry for Me Argentina." More fucking pathos.

At least now I know where he's gone.

I call the Frames and apologize for leaving. But I tell Mrs. Frame that I'm going to bring Ben home. There is a pause, and a fumble. I know that Dr. Frame has grabbed the phone from his wife. His voice shakes with anger, unction, strident disapproval.

"You need to come back immediately, Marina. Where are you? At your apartment? Are you at your apartment? The authorities are here. Not the NYPD. They are asking about you, and they are asking about Benjamin. I demand that you come back at once and answer these allegations. This is no joke, young lady. Trust me when I tell you that whatever sympathy and understanding I have for your tragedy, that does not alter one iota the fact that you are not entirely innocent in my eyes. Not as long as the authorities are here and asking after my son. They are on the way to pick you up. Wait outside your building for them."

I am hurtling down the steps, my ears full of the squeal of a Manhattan-bound train entering the station, when I run smack into Sonya Moiseevna from downstairs.

"*Gospodi bozhe moy*," she gasps. "What on earth has been going on in your apartment! Whole brigades! Platoons of leather coated characters, clomping up the stairs since last evening. I don't like the look of a single one. Dear God, I tell you, I was afraid to come out and even check on you, you poor thing. The faces that streamed by, God forgive me. And then Raisa calls and tells me of the chaos across the street. Oh my weak heart, poor girl is it true? Your poor Papa is dead . . . come in, God protect us, before they . . . where are you going? Marina!" She is shrieking, just like the horrified survivors of the body-snatchers, and I am hardly touching the steps, half way across the street, rushing up the steps to the elevated tracks.

"Well, go then, you heedless girl! Run back to where you and father, that *vor*, came from and take your good-for-nothing, reprobate uncle with you!"

I hurdle the turnstile and squeeze through the gap. The doors close and I am aboard the Q train, fleeing the forces that would trap me, infect me with the horror that Sonya and Raisa already see incubating.

MILTON KRESPKY LIVES ON 72nd street between Amsterdam and Columbus Avenues. I recognize the building, a faded Edwardian glory with a Gray's Papaya Hot Dog joint on the first floor. My stomach growls at the smell, reminding me that I haven't eaten in far too long. But someone is leaving Krespky's building, and I can't be sure that anyone but a stranger will let me in.

Inside the front entrance I scan the mailboxes and find Krespky—7F. My heart is like a scared rabbit as I climb the stairs. At the seventh floor landing I pause, listening to voices—women gossiping in Spanish at one end of the hall; Bob Barker at the other, inviting his next contestant to "Come on down!" Here in the middle, from behind the door of 7F, a warbling lament that I know must be making Ben grit his teeth. I'm struck by just how desperate to disappear he must be if he is willing to hide out with Krespky's show tunes.

I raise my fist to the door but hesitate, hearing footsteps from the other side. I feel an eye blink behind the peephole. I raise mine, presenting my face for scrutiny. The lock unbolts. Krespky, smaller than I remember him in his argyle vest and wide-bale corduroys, ushers me in wordlessly and locks the door behind us. A heavy curtain falls across the only window, blocking all but a sliver of daylight. A dozen lamps with battered shades compensate. Next to a narrow bookshelf is an equally narrow door to an even narrower galley kitchen. A teakettle whistles on the stove. I can see the corner of a small table covered with a lace cloth. A cat winds itself around one of the legs. And then I notice another leg. Black denim and a bare foot. Ben's.

Krespky looks at me from over his narrow glasses.

"He came early this morning," he says in a low voice. "He said people would be looking for him. He didn't say it would be you."

I'm not sure whether it's derision or simple observation. Nor do I care.

Krespky walks to the stereo, turns off the music and announces, "Ben. You've been found."

Ben rises, toppling his chair, trodding on the cat. I cross the room and stand before him. His eyes are tormented. Dark iris, darker pupil, dark circles beneath. I cannot breathe. We stand looking at each other, the longest split-second in the history of the world. Then he drops to his knees, wraps his arms around my legs, and sobs.

I let him. I know he is doing it for me, crying for me. The front door opens and closes. We are alone.

I slide to the floor with him. I don't wipe the tears, neither his nor mine. I don't kiss him. I don't ask myself why I want to kiss him. I don't hit him. I don't ask myself why I don't want to hit him.

I have to start somewhere, so I say, "Why did you leave me?"

But now that I've started I can't stop. I am asking, demanding, imploring. *Why did you leave me why did you go didn't you know that I need you when you know that I'm alone and you leave me when I need you and don't you know that my father is dead and I love you and I love you and you left me so how can you leave me if you love me don't you love me?*

His answer is the hardest kiss with the softest lips. Again and again.

When he has answered that way, he says that he loves me. That he loves me more than anything, and he can't bear knowing that I love him. "Because you will stop loving me," he finishes "You will stop when you know. I will lose you, and I've only just gotten you."

His forehead is on mine and I feel his body tremble. *Prosti menya.*

"Know what?" I ask. "What is it?"

His face contorts with distress. He moves away from me and leans against the wall. His breathing is ragged.

"Tell me. My father is dead—what can you possibly have to tell me that . . ."

"I was there," he interrupts. "I was there. When your

father shot Georgi. I saw it. Lindsay and me. Oh God, she just wouldn't . . . she just went up the alley and the door was open and she . . ."

I close my eyes and listen.

As I listen I see. More clearly than a vision of the future is this story of the past: a past so present that it is now.

Ben is talking, telling me what happened less than twenty-four hours ago. Eyes closed, I see it all: I see him standing at the pay phone outside the Corsair, looking up at my apartment, hoping that I will pick up. I see him glance back at the car, where Lindsay should be waiting, but she's not. She's out of the car and halfway up the alley. She's gesturing, leaning out from between the dumpsters pushed up against the club's brick wall: *Come quick. Come see this.* I see him put down the receiver and hurry up the alley to pull her back from the violent argument inside. From my father's mouth—from the words that Lindsay doesn't understand: *Don't say that, you traitor. Don't say that, you miserable traitor. Don't say it or I swear I will kill you.* I see Ben flinch at the sound of the gun. One-two-three shots. I see him clap a hand over Lindsay's mouth, too late to stop her scream. I see all three of them now, a panicked triangle hustled and grabbing in the half-shadowed doorway, the gloom of Vova Skilarky's office not enough to obscure the horrible clarity of Gosha on the floor and Lindsay trapped by my father's forearm, his gun to her head.

I open my eyes, but they go blind as Ben says, "I knew that he could pull the trigger, Marya. I knew he would do it. He was out of his mind. And there was a gun on the floor. Gosha's. And I don't know how but it got into my hands and I swear I've never even held a gun before. I don't know who was crazier at that moment, because even though I was thinking, *he's out of his mind he'll shoot* . . . In the end, it was me. I shot. I shot your father, Marya. I killed him.'"

WHEN YOU ARE ILL and your body is fever, it is so hard to remember what healthy feels like. When you have nothing to drink in a desert, you cannot, you will not, recall what it's like not to thirst. When you are cold there is no memory of heat. And when you toss in the nighttime, sleep is a lie.

So it is in the minutes that follow, and I reject completely the possibility that I ever loved this boy. So it is a moment later when an urgent fist on the door makes clear that Krespky is not back from his errand. I look at Ben's face. I see that his agonies are gone. There is only fear. My horror is gone, too. There is only the rejection of my lie to myself. It is quick and it is thoughtless, but I have swung over an abyss and back. I will not lose another person I love.

"Who do you think is looking for you?" I ask.

"I took the disc," he answers.

"Get it now and get your shoes. We are going out the back door."

Milton Krespky's cat squeezes through the cracked-open window onto the fire escape and preens herself in the sun.

THIRTEEN
EROICA

"We should just give it to them," I say once more. "I honestly don't care what's on it. I just want them to leave us alone."

Ben pushes a strand of hair from my face. "Believe me," he says. "I'm not trying to be a hero here. Not anymore."

We peek out from our refuge, a miniature castle perched on a rock in the middle of Central Park. I guess this is what they call a "folly"—a stone and slate structure clambering up the shale, complete with towers, turrets, and terraces. In every direction, there is the park and its high-rise perimeter, beyond which lies the real world: the graffiti, the bums, the trash. Manhattan is being held at bay by a silent moat of wonder. If only that were true of the men who are looking for us.

They spotted us the minute we emerged from the

back of Krespky's building, tipped off by the one who was first into the kitchen, his head out the window as we dropped from the bottom of the fire escape.

At first they were discreet. One man, jacketless, followed us on foot while two others got in a towncar the color of eggplant and drifted slowly into the street. We sped up, supposing, strategizing. On that long block to Columbus Avenue, we hoofed it with backward glances. The one who had busted the door began to run. Then at the corner near the Science Museum, another one appeared. Short red hair, cropped close to the scalp. As he approached us we saw him pull his gun. That's when the car lurched and swerved to block our path.

We didn't really have a chance.

Except the Muse of Manhattan intervened. She sent us a dog walker fumbling with a half-dozen leashes and a cross-town bus. If we hadn't been fleeing, I might have stopped to laugh at the pratfalls in our wake: the goon entangled with the greyhounds and the hysteria of the tiny Chinese woman as she banged on the hood of the eggplant-mobile. But none of it was funny.

We ran into the quiet of Central Park at dusk, and Ben led me here to this castle on the rocks, to the covered terrace with its colonnade of arches. He pulled me into his arms, where I am now.

It feels good. Until I think. And then it feels wrong. I taste the horror of it—not who I am running from; who I ran to. I don't want to feel it, but I do. It's more than confusion. It's revulsion. Ben killed my father and I am in his arms.

I step away from him, swallowing panic. Willing it to pass before he notices.

"What is this place?"

"An old weather station, believe it or not. It looks like it should be in a fairy tale, doesn't it?"

I breathe deeply. A crescent moon hides in the still-light sky, waiting for nightfall.

"It was one of the first places my father took me when we moved here. He took me to Lincoln Center. We heard the Met Orchestra play Beethoven's *Eroica*, 'The Heroic Symphony.' Afterward he brought me here. Ever since then, every time I stand here I feel like, I don't know, Napoleon on Elba, planning his heroic return. Or maybe just . . . an invincible bassoonist."

He laughs. I smile. But only briefly. Pop never brought me anywhere in Manhattan. He never had time.

"Not today, though," adds Ben. "Today, it feels like Waterloo."

Ben's face is golden in the last rays of sunlight. He's wearing the sailor coat. The same one he wore the first time I saw him on the steps of his house on New Year's Eve. I'm hot and cold, remembering this boy when he was my hero, my piano man. I reach out and touch the wool of his sleeve.

When I do I know something for certain. He had to do it. If Ben says my father was going to kill Lindsay, then my father was going to kill Lindsay. I rub the cuff of his sleeve softly, willing it to explain, to give me more reasons. What could have made Pop so desperate? What did he say? His last words: *Don't say that, you miserable traitor.* And now I understand. Gosha was not betraying Russia. He was not betraying Pop's research secrets. He was not even betraying some cockamamie mob deal gone wrong. He had betrayed something my father valued more. Gosha had said something traitorous. The same thing he had said to me at Alyona's the day before Pop died. He had said, "Sveta's dead."

I had run away when he said that. My father had lost his mind.

I plunge my hands all the way into Ben's coat and hold onto him. "Please," I say into his collarbone. "Please let's get free of this. Let's just call the man from the, what is it called? The one who told me Skilarsky has an alibi?"

"FBI. The FBI deals with domestic crime. Like the mob. And like espionage." I blink away the last notion. My father as a spy.

"So they can use this. They want a reason to lock up the *bratva*. They can take the disc and arrest these guys who are after us, no?"

He laughs. There's no humor in it. "It never works that way in the movies."

We are quiet. A siren wails. "I can't win this one," he says. "Even if you forgive me. You can't protect me. If we give the disc to the authorities those thugs will just come to my house. They may be there now, Marya. My parents could be in danger."

"Thugs." Ben used the American word. He didn't call them *kholodilniki* or *dubinki*. And I realize he's right. Those men who followed us . . . they were quiet. They were well dressed. None of them wore leather. None of them cursed. Even when they got entangled, and we gave them the slip, not a single *whore* or *bitch*.

It dawns on me like fool's gold: those men were not Russian. They were not sent by Vova Skilarsky.

They may be there now.

"Oh God, Ben."

I back away again, this time with alarm.

"I led them straight to you. Those men weren't *bratva*. They were the same men who came to your house after I left this morning. Your father said they were asking about you and then he said they were coming to my apartment to get me. Ben, they must have tailed me. And now that they've put us together . . ."

Ben is trying to understand.

"Not *bratva*?" he asks.

I shake my head. "CIA."

Neither of us says what we are thinking. Men who chase you with guns are bad guys. I think back to Sergei's warning: *The Frames—they are implicated.* I hear Ben's father's voice again on the phone, perhaps more frightened than angry. They've threatened Dr. Frame. I cover my mouth, horrified by what I've done. I've brought ruin on his family. I've made his father vulnerable.

But then, he has killed mine.

Maybe we're even.

• • •

I'M SURPRISED WHEN SERGEI answers on the first ring.

"I have your disc. Now call off your friends," I say in English.

"Marina. Are you okay?"

"I want to make a deal," I tell him, switching to Russian. "You get the disc, but you have to guarantee immunity for Ben. You have to expunge the Frames' name from anything incriminating. Anywhere: on the record, or in your files, anywhere at all. And you have to call off these people who are chasing us."

I'm breathing heavily. The smell of duck roasting in the musty Chinese restaurant is making my head spin. At least we found a pay phone where it's warm. Right near the toilet.

"Wait a minute," says Sergei. "Who's chasing you? Where? When?"

"You tell me. The same four guys who interrogated Dr. Frame today demanding to know where to find me and find Ben. Them. Only up here. Near Juilliard. Not an hour ago. They didn't even bother to ask if we had it. They broke the damn door, Sergei! They have guns!"

"Slow down," he says. "I need you to slow down. Wait a second, just hold on. I need to get on another phone. *Do not* hang up."

I wait for a second. A minute. I'm getting nervous, imagining the recording machines he's putting into gear. I'm about to hang up when he comes back on the line and says: "Listen closely. I can't talk long. You have to listen and you have to trust me. This morning when I came to see you, I was not authorized. They don't know I was there. I hoped that you would give me the disc because I don't want it getting into their hands. They aren't after state secrets, Marya. They are playing a game. A war game. Not about real war, biological or chemical. This is about fabricating a paper trail that makes US intelligence look smarter than KGB. Pure and simple. They are using you to entrap Dr. Frame. They will make him a fall guy. A mole."

"He's an academic," I say. "You're lying."

"It doesn't matter if I am. It doesn't matter *who* lies. If they succeed, he will be a spy. Don't you get it? He will be the turned agent they can blame for a decade's worth of sloppy work, leaks, failed operations. Do you understand? They don't need much at all."

I am silent for a moment, reliving that sinking feeling I got when I understood that Sergei was not KGB, that he would not be handing over my mother in exchange for my father's information. It's the same thing all over again. Sergei is another stranger. He has gone rogue—he is not the enemy, but he is also not the man who can stop the enemy. He is a good guy, and that doesn't help me right now.

"What do I do?" I ask.

"Do they know that you have it?"

"They know that we ran."

"It's too late then. You need to destroy it."

"So, you don't want it after all? It doesn't have top-secret weapons information? It's not a bomb after all?"

"Marya, I told you. It's just a trap."

"You know my father is dead because of this disc, right?"

I don't even hear Sergei's response. I'm deaf at the moment to everything but the screaming in my head. *That is not why he's dead. That is not why at all.* I know the truth. Pop is dead because he lost his mind. And he lost his mind because he lost his wife. And he lost his wife because she knew things that could very well be on that disc, whether Sergei knows that or not. But there's more. There's Lindsay and Ben, who both could have been killed. Lindsay has nothing to do with germ warfare. Ben has nothing to do with germ warfare. And now . . . I am being told that this disc has nothing to do with germ warfare. I close my eyes and remember my father on the boardwalk asking me to please find Sergei. *It's a fake*, he had said, *but when they find out . . .* What does a fake floppy disc prove? That an American academic is a double agent? Or that the KGB's weakest link is a clairvoyant ballerina?

There's no one and nothing I can believe. I place the phone gently on the hook, as if by disconnecting the call I can disconnect the whole tragicomedy that has brought me here, with a floppy disc in my hand. How many dollars does this stupid piece of plastic cost? It has already cost as many lives.

I join Ben at a small table by the window. He's bought us egg rolls. I devour one and then tell him that we need a new plan.

WE TURN OVER IDEAS and solutions like cards in a game of concentration. None of them match. Eventually I turn the Gosha card. We've not considered it yet.

"He tipped me off," I say. "Sort of. He obviously saw you . . ." I can't bring myself to say it.

"Yes. He saw me kill your father. He's a witness. He will testify. If he doesn't, he goes to jail."

My stomach roils. It's not the thought of Gosha in jail; it's the idea of Ben on trial. I remember the vision I had the night he came to me. A vision of a man with a gun. A vision of a bloody hand placed on top of a book. I've seen the courtroom dramas on TV: "Do you solemnly swear to tell the truth?" That's what they ask when you place your hand on the bible and try to explain yourself.

"But it was self-defense," I argue. "You were protecting her."

"I fled the scene. That is a crime."

"That's why we need the disc. It will buy us—something. It has to."

"It can only buy us a lie that will frame my father. I have to do this."

"Gosha," I sigh. It has to be the answer. "Gosha can prove that you had to do what you did. And he can arrange for you to be protected. You and your family." Even as I say it, I know it is not the answer.

"My family will never be protected by the *bratva*."

There's my confirmation. Even Gosha cannot solve this.

We sit in silence, defeated. He won't meet my gaze. He stands.

"I need to call my father."

For a moment I feel the slap of his voice. His father will pay for my father's crimes, one way or another. But then I remember that my father has already paid. And it was Ben who fixed the price.

BEN'S FATHER'S ANSWER IS simple: We can't know what to do until we confirm what is on the disc. If it is real, we must protect it. If it is bogus, we expose it. He tells Ben to wait, not to move. He's driving in.

"Be careful," warns Ben. "We don't know who is looking for us. Or you."

By the time Dr. Frame arrives it is nearly nine o'clock. He embraces his son, hard and fierce. I don't know how much Ben has told him about why he didn't come home or why he has the disc. But when Dr. Frame turns to me and grabs me just as tightly, I think he knows more than I could have told him. I'm glad when he lets go. I was afraid he would apologize, and I don't want any more apologies. Unless it is some sort of cosmic plea for forgiveness on behalf of the universe, for dealing me such a shitty hand. A promise from on high to make it all better. Without that, *prostite menya* gets me nowhere.

Dr. Frame drives us downtown to his university. He takes us up to the third floor and down a darkened hall. He flips the lights on in a large room: a computer lab. Three rows of machines blink, like humans in a dark cave, surprised by the sun. On the back wall, computer banks rise from floor to ceiling, humming, counting, storing. Spinning wheels of tape. Data. Information.

Dr. Frame sits behind a monitor and holds his hand out for the disc. We watch him slide it in. I have no idea what to expect. The computer screen goes blank and then prompts, a pale green interface. He taps, commanding the disc to give up its secrets. It doesn't comply. He scratches his head, types more commands, checks the directory files and the execution files.

Five minutes pass. Ten. He looks up at his son, beat.

Wordlessly Ben takes his place, typing short bursts like machine gun fire, intent on busting a safe. I remember Lindsay's words: *like Warren Beatty in* Bonnie in Clyde.

"The operating system doesn't recognize this code," he says. "It's not a readable file. It's encrypted."

He tries a few more commands in a language I know nothing of. This is not English or Russian. Not graffiti or jive. Not the crude language of *bratva*, and not the French of ballet.

"I can't hack it," says Ben.

Dr. Frame walks to the phone on the wall and dials the operator. "I need Misha Komarsky," he says. "Try the engineering library."

Twenty minutes later a student named Misha is hunched over the keyboard, cracking the code that I pray will set us free. He is pale, short, and fat. He wears a grimy white lab coat over a black T-shirt speckled with what might be Dorito dust.

The room grows warm.

"This is going to be an all-nighter," Misha says.

I am shocked to learn that, if nothing else, my father knows how to bury a body. He's locked his secrets in the finest Soviet encryption.

"We'll stay," says Dr. Frame.

FOURTEEN
AND THAT IS ALL

It's past midnight when I awake. I'm lying on a couch in the corner of the computer lab, my head on Benjamin's knee. I don't move. I just lie there feeling his fingers run through my hair, watching the hand of the clock jerk in minute increments. Misha is still hunched over the keyboard. I close my eyes again, wanting nothing but this silence and Ben's fingers. I feel a shudder run through his body. And then another one. I know what this is. I sit upright and cradle his head to my shoulder where he can muffle his crying.

"Don't," I whisper.

His shoulders heave again.

"Or do. It's fine. I just mean . . . don't think about whatever it is you are thinking. If you are thinking about the Corsair—don't. If you are thinking that you did something wrong, stop."

He covers his eyes with his hand, trying to control himself.

"I don't even remember picking it up," he chokes. "The gun. I don't remember firing. It's like I was temporarily insane. Me, Marya. Insane."

"No," I say. "Don't say that. We both know who the insane one was in that room. Don't confuse what you prevented with what you did."

I pull his hand from his eyes and kiss his palm. A second of doubt—*Did he really put a gun to her head?*— flies through my mind and is gone, chased by the vision I had in Lansky's, of the man with the gun and the terror on Lindsay's face.

I swing my legs to the floor, and still holding Ben's head, lie back against the other end of the couch. I pull him with me until we are face-to-face, on the same level, prone and vulnerable.

"I would do anything to take it back. To rewind the clock," he whispers.

"I know."

I wrap my arms around him. I wrap my legs around him. I wrap my heart around him.

"It won't end like this," I say. "This will end differently. I don't know how exactly, but it will end. And when it does, we can talk about the past and the future. But right now is just this present."

He raises his eyes to mine. He is searching, and I think he can hear what I can't say. That I will forgive him. That I love him. He kisses my lips. Then my eyes and my hair and my hands. Then he collapses in my arms and falls asleep.

I wait until his breathing slows, until the line of pain

between his eyes disappears. Then I cover my eyes with my arm and and let the world go dark. For the first time in my life I deliberately beckon a vision of the future. And in it I see Sveta. Alive. Free. I see the flair of her skirt as she pirouettes against the sunset. Behind her are the black silhouettes of Coney Island's roller coasters.

WHEN I AWAKE AGAIN it is not to the sensation of Ben's fingers in my hair. It is to the unwelcome racket of feet, fast and aggressive, running down the hallway outside. My eyes snap open. Ben jumps from my lap. Dr. Frame tips over a chair. Misha rises slowly, his hands in the air.

"*Dobroe utro*," growls Vova Skilarsky. It is not. A good morning. Not at all. It is not even morning. *When they find out . . .* His two beefy henchmen step into the lab, guns cocked.

More fucking guns. The sight of them throws me into a panic.

But Dr. Frame keeps his cool as he explains the situation. "The disc is encrypted. You will need our assistance to break it, but then I am sure we can come to an arrangement."

Skilarsky cracks his knuckles. He cracks his neck. He was not prepared for this turn of events. He responds accordingly: *son of a whore*. And then, remarkably, he sits down to wait.

I rise. I feel Ben grab my wrist but I shake it off and go to stand in front of Vova Skilarsky.

"Was it Levshik?" I ask.

His craggy brow darkens.

"Did Georgi Levshik tell you where to find us?" I demand.

"That *mudak*." Skilarsky sneers. "*Nyet, devushka.* He buttoned up tight that one. He's got about five fewer teeth than he did last night, but it didn't make him any chattier."

"Then how," I begin.

"Freeze—FBI!"

Here is my answer, shouted from the doorway.

"I stay one step ahead of the wolves," says Skilarsky, an ugly slow smile creeping across his scarred face.

Skilarsky's guys are ready for this second wave of men. "G-men," I remember. They are called G-men in the gangster movies. Government men, with their shiny shoes and their badges and hats. These guys don't look like the movies, but they are FBI, and they have found us, too, in this dark hour before dawn.

"Oy," whispers Misha in apology to Ben's father. "I had to call my buddy for the last level of encryption. Um. He's an FBI guy . . . I didn't really expect this kind of service."

You might think that this is the climax. The denouement. One of those moments in that my brief five weeks in Bay High's literature class has hinted at. The moment when it all comes to a point.

But it's not. Because even as I watch the *bratva* raise their handguns like the hairs on their neck and the G-men, the FBI, shift and bristle in their shoes, with their guns trained on the mobsters . . . there is more. There are more voices and more men and more elbows.

There are badges and blusters and loud male warnings: *"Back down back the fuck down"* and four more men.

One of them is the redheaded crew cut. A-ha. Good. Now all of the players are here.

I sink to my knees. *Stop, drop and roll.* Ben drags me back toward the couch, out of the half-dozen lines of fire that have suddenly been made manifest in this computer lab in Dr. Frame's university, where Misha Komarsky is just one layer away from breaking the most sophisticated data block he has encountered in his undergraduate career.

Dr. Frame speaks. The room listens but the guns are not lowered. "We just need to deactivate the magnetic tape and insert an acoustic strip."

The crew cut nods. "Break it," he says. "Break it now."

I am watching this standoff: nine men, armed, bristling, and clueless. They have no idea what to expect, what they are after. Only that they are here to prevent, to acquire, to get.

And the absurdity, this unlikely situation where all of the players have been scattered across the chessboard, brings clarity: I was wrong all along. I'd thought that this whole tragedy was caused by something bigger than me. Bigger than Ben. Bigger even than my father and Sveta and Gosha and the delusions they have nursed since Moscow became their prison. I thought it was bigger than Lukino. Bigger than my father's work and my mother's gift and the unhappy consequences of that combination.

But it's not.

It's smaller than any of that.

It is smaller than the terrible stockpiles of weapons these two countries are building in the name of peace. It is smaller than the crack in history that you can fall on the wrong side of. It is smaller than Dr. Frame's accomplishments, smaller than Gosha's dreams. It is smaller than my forgiveness of Ben. And it is certainly smaller than my father's love. His tragic, pathetic love.

It's men following orders like dogs chase their tails.

I wait, the seconds like hours. Who will be able to explain this to all the men in this room, men determined not to lose? Men who must get something, extract something, and carry it away like a trophy. Who will tell them what is really at stake? What all this is worth? Who will tell them there is nothing here but a dead man's broken heart?

In the end, it is the computer itself. Stripped of its encryption, the disc doesn't simply reveal. It sings. *Pereski morya i okeany. Cross the ocean, but do not cross time. This is why I have left you behind. This is all I have left for you. Vot tak, i vsyo. And that is all.*

Every face in the room registers incomprehension. Except for mine. I know every word. This is my music. This is my salve. This is my father's message to me. All that he's left me.

"What the hell?" asks the crew cut "That's it?"

Misha Komarsky rubs his eyes and nods. *Vot tak, i vsyo.* That is all.

This is all. This is Winged Guitars.

• • •

"NOTHING BUT MUSIC?" LINDSAY asks. "Was it at least, you know, a code? Some kind of backwards message? Like Paul is Dead. How do you say Die Capitalist Pigs backward in Russian?"

Benjamin Frame, musical and mathematical wunderkind, says it: "*Yenivs khiksechilatipak irmu.*"

Lindsay rolls her eyes. "Jeez," she says.

"I know, right?"

And that is our little fugue:

Jeez.

I know.

Can you believe it?

That's all.

That's all it was.

Vot tak, i vsyo.

Outside it is twilight, but I can hardly keep my eyes open. Ben sees.

"We should get home," he says.

He stands and kisses Lindsay on the head. He holds her face for a moment in his hands. I see the fatigue and the sadness cloud his eyes. "I am going in tomorrow. To turn myself in." Her face drops. She had nearly forgotten. "They will book me. Hold me for I don't know how long. But they'll let me out on bail. And then." Ben looks at me. What he is saying is for me to hear, too. "Then there will be a trial and you and Marya will both be there to speak on my behalf. And they won't throw the book at me. I hope."

Lindsay grabs his hands with her own. "Of course they won't, Ben. You were a hero. A true, you know, knight, Good Samaritan, Sumerian, whatever." She glances at me and flushes red. Knights slay dragons. Heroes kill monsters.

I wonder if it will ever be the same. It won't, of course. I will be grateful if it just *is*. Different is fine, as long as it can still *be*. Me and Lindsay. Me and the girl who stepped on that last straw and broke it. She had already explained, asked my forgiveness. Not for wandering into that alley. But for staying away from me all that long night afterward. She had been with Ben, she explained. And when she left him, close to sunrise at Milton Krespky's doorstep, he was still desperate. *She can't know that it was me. She can never find out it was me.* She had promised Ben, she explained.

"He was more terrified of you finding out than he was of the cops. It's true, Marya. That boy is crazy, crazy in love."

I understand where her loyalties lie. Ben is her oldest friend. I am the reason he asked her to lie. I know I should be grateful that I am somewhere among them, these problematic loyalties.

Now I turn my back on them both. I can't face any more regret, any more guilt. I'm in the hallway putting on my coat when she comes out, too, and puts her arms around me from behind. I freeze.

"You are one crazy hardluck case, Marina Ivanova," she says. Her voice trembles. "Let me tell you, girl, if I didn't know better, I would envy you. No. I do know better, and I still envy you. You have that thing. That beautiful and brave thing. I hope you will let me stay near it. Admire it. That thing you have."

And then she's gone. Back into the kitchen clattering dishes. Ben helps me with my coat and follows me out into a clear black night.

The worst is over. Well, maybe not the worst. But the unknown. After the anti-climax in the computer lab, we were taken to FBI headquarters. The crew cut threw a manila envelope, labeled EXHIBIT A, onto a messy desk. Exhibit A was the floppy desk: the most elaborately packaged Russian ballad New York's intelligence organs have ever encountered. Exhibit A in the acquittal of Dr. Frame and the bluff of Viktor Dukovsky.

We were there for hours. Ben gave a statement; Dr. Frame called lawyers, signed affidavits, gave credentials, references, collateral. At one point I spied Sergei answering the crew cut's questions. I rose to meet him, maybe even thank him. But his eyes warned me. Told me to stay in the clear while I could. I sat back down and watched him exit stage right, his last dance a walk-off. I hoped he was free.

I heard various people talking about Georgi. "Levshik will have to corroborate. Levshik was a decoy. Levshik's bogus, not a player. Skilarsky himself has disavowed him."

They had ignored me. That was fine. Though if they had known what I was thinking—if they had known that the blown-up bogus disc had made space in my head to remember something else, something real: the handwritten notes brought from Moscow, from beyond

Moscow, from Lukino, from a psych ward. If they had known that, I might not have been ignored.

But I had said nothing about that. That is a discussion just for Gosha and me. When he is ready to take notes about what *I* have seen: My mother. Alive. Free.

Ben and I walk now in silence, not knowing where to start.

Finally I speak. Answering Lindsay though she can no longer hear: "Not Marina Ivanova."

"What?" Ben asks.

"I was talking to Lindsay. I'm not Marina Ivanova. My name is Marina Dukovskaya."

Ben takes my hand. "It's good to meet you, Marina Dukovskaya. May I call you Marya?"

THE NEXT MORNING I arrive early at the hospital and take the elevator to the third floor. There is a different cop.

"What happened to the other guy?" I ask. "He maybe fall asleep on job?"

"Something like that, yeah."

Gosha is asleep. I stand by his head, waiting. His eyes flutter open.

"Will you testify?" I ask.

"So direct, you've become," he answers. He sits up, rubs sleep from his eyes, the corner of his mouth. It's true; he's been beaten around the face. Teeth are missing. There are holes in his grimace. "Bring me some water, would you?"

I bring him a glass.

"How are you feeling?" I ask.

"Like a million bucks," he says in English.

"Is that what the disc was worth?"

"Oy, Marya. Such judgment."

He drinks. The whole glass. Rests back against the pillow. I wait for him to speak.

"You didn't tell them," I say. "You didn't tell them that Ben took the disc."

"*Gospodi*, Marya," he sighs. "Haven't I done enough without ratting out your boyfriend?"

"They found us anyway," I tell him. "So did the FBI. Skilarsky is in the slammer."

Gosha's look is surprise. He sits up higher.

"The disc was garbage." I say. "Pop had nothing."

He rubs his mouth again, unsure how to react.

"How could you be so stupid, Gosha?" I ask. It comes out nastier than I want it to. "How could you fall for it, too?"

He's gone, the man with all the answers. In his place is a man afraid of the questions I have.

"What did you fight about? What did you say that made him crazy?" I ask. I know the answer. But I need to hear him confess. I need him to be accountable for once in his life.

He takes his glasses off and rubs his eyes. "I said that the KGB had killed Sveta. It was a desperate thing to say. But I thought that he would do it. I thought he would give them a terrible weapon. And Marya, I may not know what has or will become of your mother. But I know that Moscow is no Motherland. It is evil. An evil force in the world."

"And Pop heard both those things. That both Sveta and his country are dead to him. So he called you a traitor and he shot you."

"He did," conceded Gosha. His voice unsteady.

"And then you let Ben go, with the disc, and you refused to say . . ."

"I was afraid that Skilarsky would find him. Damnit, Marya—I saw what a mess I had made. I saw it. And all I wanted after that was to protect you and the boy."

"You were so wrong, Gosha." Now it is my voice that trembles.

"It is, as I told you, a *pateticheskaya* sonata," Gosha sighs. Our silence is painful.

"Do you know that Tchaikovsky died eight days after he completed that symphony?" he asks, finally. "The Pathetique?"

I shake my head. There are tears in my eyes.

"They call it the suicide symphony. Maybe he did. Maybe he didn't. It is one of my favorites. Dark. But lovely. And written for love. They say that, too. Written with love for his nephew."

Gosha reaches over to a tray near his bed and pulls a tissue from the box. He waves it at me.

He says, "I don't have a nephew."

I step closer to Dyadya Gosha. My uncle.

"We need you," I say. "You haven't earned an easy out."

Gosha lifts his eyes and says, "I know that, *dochka*. I know."

I stand watching him for a long time. Somewhere in there is the best man at my parent's wedding. The man who will testify that Ben shot my father in self-defense. The uncle who loves me. Loves my mother and my father. I will bring him back.

"Sveta is alive, Gosha," I say. "I know it is true. Not all is lost. *Ne vsyo.*"

He nods. He struggles to speak. I wait for him to say it: "*Nyet. Ne vsyo.* Not all."

He's made me believe it. That he trusts me. I lean down and kiss his cheek, and then I leave.

THE SUN IS HIGH when I reach the boardwalk. It is still a long walk home, but I have time before I need to be there, to accompany the Frames to the precinct house where Ben will turn himself in.

"I'm going with you," I had told him last night as we lay together in his bed.

"And I'm going with you," he had answered.

"Go where? When?"

"Wherever and whenever. When I am free. Wherever we need to go to get her. Your mother." I had told him about the vision—my mother on the boardwalk. I know that this vision of the future is real. And I'm not frightened.

I think of the promises Pop made. *He would make it right. He would bring her home.* Even when I believed him, his promises scared me. As though he were swearing to raise the dead. But he is gone, and so is my fear. In its place is something like a map, or a compass—something that I know will get me to her, across oceans, with time. That is what he has left me. It's all that he has left me.

I'm singing softly. "Cross *the ocean but do not cross time . . .*" But singing is not enough. I drop the words and, humming my own accompaniment, I dance. I dance for my father and for Sveta and for Gosha. I dance for Ben.

Brighton, my new stage, beckons. But something makes me linger, soaking up the sun glinting of the ridge of Coney Island's American mountains. That's what we call roller coasters in Russian—*American mountains.* I hear again her message to me, as she danced in my head on the boardwalk: *I will climb those American mountains. Yes, me, an old lady, I will ride those roller coasters with you, my Marya.*

I wait. To see. If the slim figure below the Parachute Jump, the one getting larger with each beat of my heart, could be a strong woman in a shabby *dublonka . . .*

Because stranger things have happened: I have crossed oceans and, for better or worse, I have crossed time. But now I will wait. I won't be left behind. *Vot tak, i vsyo.* And that is all.

ACKNOWLEDGMENTS

Thanks to Dan, without whom there would be no story. To Sunita, without whom there would be no title. And to ДДТ, without whom there would be no music.